ONE BOY, ONE PONY, TWO GIRLS

BILL SPIES

The Reading Glass Books
1-888-420-3050
www.readingglassbooks.com
fulfillment@readingglassbooks.com

TABLE OF CONTENTS

Chapter 1

A HISTORY BEGUN (CIRCA AD 1500)

Hi, I am a two-year-old tricolor paint filly. I was born and raised on a large, beautiful hacienda in Spain that was owned by a nice Catholic family. Most of them know some of our language. They are very kind and gentle. We call them and their kind two-legs-no-feathers. They call us horses. We understand a few of their words and actions, but they know little to nothing about how we communicate to each other. Two-legs-no-feathers act as though they are the only ones who can talk to each other. We know by the sounds of their voices, actions, and odors when they are demanding, kind, angry, or afraid. Only very few two-legs-no-feathers understand us and how we talk to each other.

We notice many things that they just do not get. We use all our senses to communicate with each other. We can smell water, food, fear, danger, and many odors in the air. We see in the day and in the night. Certain movements of our nostrils, eyes, ears, tails, and feet relay messages to others. Movements of our heads and of our entire bodies are clear signals and signs to those who are wise to our ways. We hear what is taking place around us. We hear the two-legs-no-feathers when they call us to come to them. We hear each other's snorts of danger or to caution us. Nicker, whinny, neigh, and bugle are ways we use our voices to talk.

We enjoy certain touches, such as scratching our backs, and we have other parts, such as our ears and face, we prefer left untouched until we know you. We scratch each other and ourselves by using our teeth, and sometimes we scratch ourselves using a hind foot. Our nostrils and mouths are super sensitive to touches. That is how we find grasses among the thorns both day and night.

We also use taste to tell us what may be good or bad to eat. Horses communicate using many things, not just sound and sight. We watch what other animals do and learn from them. While some two-legs-no-feathers know a few of our ways of communicating, many do not even have a clue. Yet they call us dumb animals because they believe we cannot talk! Oh, how I wish we horses could communicate with all two-legs-no-feathers!

My mother is a beautiful dappled-gray full-blooded Arabian. She came from Syria. My mom is fast and can run for hours on end. She has a core of toughness, and she does not allow anyone or anything to push her around. She is the leader of our herd. She leads us to the coolest water, to the best places to graze, and to the nicest shady spots. We move and stop as she directs.

My dad is a powerful satin-black half-Andalusian, part-Lusitano, and part-Barb. Some claim the Barb horses are just another strain of the Arabians. That may be true. He charges around like he is some kind of a big-time war horse. Mom pays little attention to him until he gets on her nerves. When she has enough of his antics, she lays her ears back, charges him, and usually ends up giving him a nip on his neck or hip. He hardly ever gets away soon enough to dodge her dart-like attack. Her attacks please him to no end. He will romp and spring into the air, shaking his head, then prance around, showing how he enjoyed every minute of it. He and all of us know who the boss is: my mom!

I have Dad's muscles and size, Mom's keen head, slender neck, and legs, and Mom's speed and endurance. My color came from only God knows where—just the combination of my family background, I guess. I am the only paint I have ever seen. Sometimes that makes me feel special, and other times it is embarrassing. The two-legs-no-feathers who know me come often to pet and scratch me. They offer me fruits and tender vegetables while not doing much with any of the other horses. That is embarrassing!

I'll share with you how I came to be in America. One day in midsummer, a couple of two-legs-no-feathers, complete strangers, came out on the range with the range foreman of our hacienda. They walked around us peeping and peering at every detail of all us young horses. Sometimes they acted angry toward our owner, shouting and shaking their fists. Finally, they came closer to me and made me run around a little. They shook hands with one another and left.

The next day, one of the strangers and two others returned riding horses. I could tell they were not nice two-legs-no-feathers as were those of our hacienda. They rode close to me, and before I knew what was up, two of them lassoed me. They dragged me through the big front gate and on down the road. I can still hear my mom and dad bugling for me to come back. The ropes and the two horses pulling me were just too strong. I could not get away.

It was a hot, dusty road as we ambled along until late afternoon. Through the early evening dusk, I could hardly make out the individual houses up ahead. Stacked next to each other are barns and sheds. They were a gigantic forest of barns. Just past them was the biggest pond I had ever seen. I could not see the far side of it. I could smell the water. It had a funny, tangy odor, not sweet like the streams and ponds on the hacienda. It never stopped moving, even in the quiet evening.

I noticed a large herd of horses of all descriptions crammed together inside a pen made of poles. The pen full of horses was surrounded by houses. They led me to the pole fence, dropped several of the poles, whipped some of the horses close to me to make them push against the crowd, and then shoved me to make me step over the downed poles. Once I was inside, they replaced the poles, slipped the ropes off my neck, and left. I thought I would perish from thirst.

The pen was dusty, the odor so bad I could hardly breathe, and the horses crammed me against the poles covered with splinters. If I had known what I was going to endure later, I would have broken those poles or climbed over them and somehow broken away. I noticed that we kept moving slowly in a circle around the pen. There was a commotion a little way in front of me. I learned that there was a wooden barrel that had a thin little stream of water barely trickling into it.

One of the biggest stallions, a dark bay Arabian with a star on his forehead—I called him Mean Eyes—refused to leave the barrel. An assertive and regal mare pushed ahead. I called her Soft Muzzle, as she had earlier nudged me away from the splinter-covered fence, slipped between me and the rough poles, and invited me to stay next to her. She was a beautiful sorrel (about the color of an orange) Barb, with a blaze face and four white socks. Her mane and tail were a noticeably light orange color, almost white.

She moved with dignity and purpose. She fixed her eyes on Mean Eyes, laid her ears back, and struggled to get to him. He was no fool! He knew what was coming and forced himself into the crowd, allowing us to move toward the barrel. Each horse took a deep drink and moved on. The water trickling into the barrel was warm, but it quenched my burning thirst. I took a long, slow draw. My life was saved! I meandered along with the herd, anxiously waiting for my next turn at the barrel of life.

The next day, a group of the ugliest two-legs-no-feathers I have ever seen came yelling and screaming at us. Each had a long, leather whip, which they cracked and snapped as they yelled. Some had short knives hung on a belt. Others had a pistol stuck in their belt. Every once in a while, they would pop one of us with the whip and nearly draw blood. They struck the fear of death in all of us! They lowered the rails and herded us toward the big pond at the end of the road.

I saw what looked like a giant funny-shaped goose, made from brown boards, as it floated on the pond. It was long and shaped something like a huge cucumber. Its back was almost flat with some low rails around it. There were three tall trees sticking up from its back. One was close to the breast. The tallest tree was in the middle. The shortest one was close to the tail. The trees had no leaves, only short limbs sticking out both sides. Each limb had a big, white blanket (the two-legs-no-feathers called it a sail) piled on top of its entire length. The limbs (the two-legs-no-feathers called them spars) had big, long vines (the two-legs-no-feathers called them ropes) hanging from them. Also, there were several vines from the side-rails up to the top of each tree.

An AD 1500 Spanish galleon

The odor from the pond was pleasantly tangy, quite different from the sweet pools back home. There was a heavy door, hinged at the bottom, in the side of the goose. It formed a bridge from the side of the goose to the road. The two-legs-no-feathers forced us on to the bridge and into the goose. The heavy door was then bolted shut and sealed with tar. The goose (two-legs-no-feathers called it a ship) rocked and bounced all the time.

If we had not been packed so tight, we would have had trouble standing up. I thought we had been pressed tight in the pole pen! Now we were so packed that there was no space between any of us. Quickly it turned hot and steamy with an odor that was stifling. Soon, other two-legs-no-feathers arrived dressed a lot different than the ones who drove us from the pen. They wore rags tied around their heads, not large sombreros. All carried long knives and a pistol. They walked on the top of the ship, which was the roof over our heads. They called themselves sailors. A couple of them removed parts of the roof (hatches) above our heads opening three big square holes above us. The fresh air was a welcome relief! It wasn't long until they hoisted up to the very top of the tall trees those big blankets that had been lying along the top of the logs.

Soon, a slight breeze moved the big, wooden goose out onto the big pond. We could hear the wind as it pushed us along. The gentle sound of the water moving along the sides was pleasant. Before nightfall, we could no longer get glimpses through a few small cracks of the houses and trees because the pond had covered over them. The water never stopped rolling, and the ship constantly rocked.

Just before dark, the sailors threw grass on our backs. We had to snatch patches of it to eat before it fell on the floor. All of us were hungry. A wild scramble broke out by many who could not control themselves. A few of the older mares soon put a stop to all that pushing and shoving as that had caused the grass to fall on the floor. The floor was already wet from urine and manure. Also, if you lowered your head to eat, you may not find room to lift it back up before all the grass was gone because we were packed so tight. By being patient and still, I could snip pieces of grass from the backs of those next to me.

Getting a drink took sheer strength and solid determination. There was a small watering trough nailed to each side of the room we were in. Three times each day, several two-legs-no-feathers drained water from a barrel and divided it between the two troughs. Those who could not get to the trough in time to get water during the pouring would push, wiggle, and squirm, forcing themselves up the trough so they could drink the next time water was available. We never drank our fill. We were thirsty all the time.

Hours turned into days, and days became weeks. Some weakened and fell. They soon died in misery. The two-legs-no-feathers would climb over us that were still standing, tie ropes to the fallen one, and hoist the poor deceased animal up through the roof. They then slid them overboard.

The summer heat was relentless. Most of the very youngest and a couple of the very oldest horses perished from lack of food and water. That did allow us a little more room and made it easier to get to water. However, now that we had more room, it became more difficult to remain standing on the stinking, slippery floor when the wind caused the ship to violently roll and pitch.

When the wind blew hard, the ship listed sharply, and the pond water sprayed over us. It felt cool and sooo good! When the wind blew exceptionally hard, the holes above us were covered (the hatches were battened down). Then the heat sapped our strength. That, combined with the rocking and pitching, caused some to lose the ability to stand. They too soon died. Never were we treated kindly. We stayed thirsty and hungry. When the dead horses were removed, the two-legs-no-feathers beat, punched, and poked us as if it was our fault that they had to hoist them up through the hatches and slide them over the side.

After several weeks of sailing, the storms came more often. The two-legs-no-feathers became angrier and meaner. They constantly yelled at each other. Every day, it seemed to get hotter. Life on that ship was not good.

One morning, the air was different and much cooler. The clouds scurried extremely low above us. They were dark and rolled and twisted as they scudded across the sky. The wind began blowing harder and harder. The waves grew higher, with white foam blowing off their tops. A mist of cool, salty water constantly sifted through the cracks above us and soon had us soaked to the skin. The big blankets (sails) were pulled down and tied to the logs. The very front sail, called the jib, was made very small.

The two-legs-no-feathers tied ropes to the four corners of another blanket they called a canvass, and placed it on the roof at the very back of the ship.

When the storm grew worse, this canvas, called a sea anchor, was thrown overboard to be dragged behind the ship as the fierce winds blew the ship along. The sea anchor keeps the boat from getting sideways between the gigantic waves, causing it to capsize. As the waves grew higher, it began to rain. The hatches were battened down. The wind began to howl and scream worse than a pack of hungry wolves.

The ship pitched and rolled. We would rock side to side until we thought the ship would go bottom up. Thank God the two-legs-no-feathers had sense enough to put that sea anchor overboard. Thus, it kept the stern facing the large waves and the wind, so the ship was not broadsided by large waves and capsized.

We felt like we were riding on a flying eagle as the ship shot up, up, and up until we felt as though we were up in the clouds. Then it would make a sharp tip downward, and then down, down, down we would careen, headfirst, like a hawk diving to catch a rabbit. Just as we knew we must have slipped to the very bottom of the angry sea, *spaloosh*! It clapped like soft thunder! The ship shuttered and shook. Timbers groaned and screeched while water pelted down on our roof. Some horses went into hysterics—whinnying, bugling, and kicking, trying to break out. Others were so scared they just jumped up and down until they fell and eventually died.

The two-legs-no-feathers were nowhere to be heard or seen. Out of fright, the two-legs-no-feathers had crawled into any cuddy they could find. All of us were bruised, cold, hungry, thirsty, and scared to death! This wild ride continued well into the night. Suddenly, the wind stopped blowing. It kept raining. While the waves got a little smaller, they remained extremely high and rough. A couple of two-legs-no-feathers, carrying lanterns, came, gave a quick look around and left. They offered no food or water. Rain and seawater were now up to our fetlocks.

Not long after the two-legs-no-feathers left, the wind suddenly began to blow from the opposite direction from where it had been

blowing just as fiercely as ever. We now believed that we would never
see daylight again. More water began coming in through the sides. In
a very short time, the water was up to our knees.

Suddenly, I felt as though the ship bumped ever so slightly into
something just as it bottomed out between two waves. It was a strange
and eerie feeling. Up, up we went, tipped over and down, down we
fell, as we had done many of times. I waited for the bump to come
again. Nothing happened! The sequence of up, up, up, tip over, and
fall down, down, down, was followed again and again. I knew I had felt
something strange several sequences ago of the ups and downs. I stayed
alert to feel it again as it made the ship shiver as we do to shake off dust.

The waves seemed to be getting closer together, but the wind
had not slackened one bit. I was leaning back as down we went when
the usual *spaloosh* came, and yes, the ship did hit something solid. A
vigorous shudder, and another sequence of up and down started. This
time, the ship hit so hard it drove most of us down to our knees and
slammed us into one pile of bodies toward the front of our stall. The
ship rocked sharply to one side before we shot back up again.

Our fears now turned into hysteria, frantic fright, and wild screams.
I believe I even heard piercing screams from the two-legs-no-feathers just
after we hit bottom. The ship rolled sharply to one side as some of the
planks along the wall split, and seawater gushed in. A couple of the hatch
covers were washed away. Water poured in through them. Once again, the
ship groaning and cracking, heaved slowly up. Listing sharply to one side,
water continued pouring in from every direction, filling the boat even as
we continued up and up. We did not go as far up as we had been going.

The ship rolled onto its side as we sped faster than ever down, down,
down and hit bottom with a thunderous crunch. Timbers from the
downward side broke and came up. Planks and boards from the ceiling
and the troughs came flying in on the front of a large gush of water. All
of us were knocked around by the water and the debris. I sucked up
a big gulp of air as I was washed upside down. I swirled around with
feet flying. The water was cold and pushed hard against my stomach.

I was trotting in the water as fast as I could. I felt as though I was going up. It was totally black. I needed to breathe, but I was underwater. My lungs were burning. I had to keep my senses about me and hold my breath. I felt that I could not hold my breath any longer when I saw light above me. I made a couple more frantic lunges, and my face broke clear of the sea. I gulped a big gush of air and swallowed some water. I quickly coughed that out and took another quick gulp, just when another gigantic wall of water came down on me.

In seconds, I burst out of that wall. I could hear nothing but the roiling sea and the screaming wind. The waves pushed me in the direction the wind was blowing. I was alive with only a few minor cuts and bruises. I was happy, no, elated to be alive! I was bewildered as to where I was and about how I would be able to stay alive.

I calmed myself down, took up a slow trot in the water, and allowed the waves and the wind to push me along. I learned that if I moved my legs in a very slow trot and relaxed as much as possible that I could keep my nose above the water except when the waves swept over me. Not knowing where I was or how long I may have to swim, I decided that I would save as much energy as I could and continue to swim until my very last bit of energy was gone.

Eventually, the winds started to subside. The waves decreased in size and grew farther apart. Breathing became easier. I felt as though I could keep this rate for a long time, thanks to the strength from Dad and the endurance from my mom. Oh! How I wished I could see them again! I was glad they were not here with me because I did not want anyone to go through what I had endured lately.

A deep chill came over me. My muscles cramped every once in a while, and ached beyond description. My joints were sore. I was so tired I felt I could easily drop off to sleep and let my body slip into the cold water. Shaking my head, I realized that I had to change my thinking. Even though it was painful, I knew that I must keep moving or perish. I decided that I would keep moving until my joints locked up and my muscles cramped up tight.

I saw that dawn was beginning. Having been wet and cold for a day and a night, I started looking forward to the coming day and, hopefully, sunshine! I was thinking that the sun would offer some much-needed warmth when my left back foot hit something! I quickly poked my right hind foot down, and it hit solid ground. My muscles were not working right, but I pushed myself along with my hind feet. Just as my front feet began touching the sandy bottom, I saw a long, hazy white line ahead of me. I could see nothing else but the white line above the waves.

I finally realized that I was seeing two white lines. One was the tops of waves and the other was sand. Then I made out a line of trees above the white lines. I tried to surge forward and learned that I could hardly hold myself up, even with the water halfway up my body. Oh no! In my weakened condition, I will not be able to stand up, let alone walk, without the water helping to hold me up! How can I ever get to that white strip of sand?

I was forced to stop walking. Standing in the water, my legs shook. The cramps were killing me. Thankfully, the waves had decreased to long swells between me and dry ground. They became crashing rolls of water at the shoreline. Slowly I gazed up and down the coast.

A few Two-legs-with-feathers were flying along over the foaming crashes of water. Nothing else was moving, and all I could hear was the dashing waves on the white sand. I must move forward. As the swells welled up under me, I staggered a few steps forward. Once the swell left me, I had to stop, brace myself, rest, and concentrate on steadying myself to remain standing.

The sun was peeping through the clouds behind me when I finally reached the cascading breakers. The warmth gave me determination. I stepped forward. *Kabloosh*! A large breaker knocked my legs from under me. I tumbled down and flopped onto my side.

The waves crashed over me. I held my breath until it passed and then sucked up a big draft of air. Breaker after breaker of waves rolled over me. I shut my eyes, held my breath. As soon as the water passed over my nose, I sucked in a long draw of air. The sun's heat was soothing. It relaxed my muscles and reduced my cramps.

I was happy to be alive, but I was extremely hungry! The breakers were no longer covering my head. They were crashing slightly behind me. I could now lay my head on the warm sand. A deep sleep overtook me.

Eventually, the heat from the sun, shining directly overhead, awoke me. The cramps were gone. The breakers were behind me. My empty belly told me to get something to eat. I tucked my legs up next to my body. My legs were stiff and sore, but I could control them. I placed my front feet out in front of me and lunged to get up. Over I tumbled. In my scrambling to stay up, I turned around and fell facing the ocean.

I gathered my strength as I rested for a while. Now, my rump was higher than my shoulders. I had to get up! So, with both front feet placed out in front of me, I forced my front end up, waited a few seconds to steady myself, and with every ounce of strength left, I slowly pushed my backend up. My legs and joints were stiff and sore, but I had no cramps.

Moving one foot at a time, I methodically turned around and, very slowly, taking one short step at a time, I moved toward the woods. As I walked, I gained some strength. When I reached the edge of the woods, I noticed a luscious patch of grass, just past some brush and vines, growing around a springhead of fresh running water. I was determined to get to that sweet water and the grass. After nibbling a few leaves from the vines and gathering strength, I staggered through the vines and brush.

The ground beside the spring was soft. My front feet sank in up to my knees. That helped steady my body and made it easier for me to reach the clear, cool, fresh water. I drank until it hurt. While standing in the mud, I bit off and ate all the grass I could reach. I took another drink and tried to move back. Down I went on my rump. My front feet sucked loose from the mud, and I rolled on to my side. My head felt as if it were as heavy as my body. It flopped down on the mat of grass.

My thirst was quenched, my belly had food in it, and my energy was completely gone. Deep sleep totally consumed me.

Chapter 2

AN ALIEN ARRIVES

Flip flop, flip flop, flip flop. The noise of the bear-hide door flapping at the entrance woke me. My name is Tangtok, meaning "Like panther," because Father says I am fast and strong. I am of the Assateague people. We live on a long, narrow strip of land with Big Water on the side Bright Light God climbs over each morning and Little Water is on the side he hides under as it grows dark.

All day yesterday, the Wind Goddess showed her anger. The Storm God also displayed his displeasure by pushing large, dark storm clouds to blank out Bright Light God. Then came Rain God. Then Dark Goddess blanketed the earth, Storm God increased his power and released both Wind Goddess and Rain God to show their full power. Something terrible had riled them up to a ferocious frenzy. Now Mother Earth and all she had must pay for a transgression.

My father had used green vines to tie the door tightly shut, from bottom to top, before the family crawled onto our sleeping mounds. The sleeping mounds are made with tree boughs and cattail stalks as the base. Then a layer of leaves were topped with long grass. The sleeping blankets and covers were made of the very finest tanned rabbit, raccoon, and bobcat furs.

The hut shuddered and trembled as the gods raged and pounded it with powerful gusts of wind and a constant heavy downpour. My family built the house of sticks, grass, bark, and mud with four corners to make it strong and easy to make the slanted roof. That is the reason our tribe is known as the Pointy Assateague people. The other tribe, who lives two Bright Light walks away, is the Roundy Assateague, or Chincoteague, people. Their huts are round, like a tree. Their village is on the highest ground of another island that is very close to Assateague.

A typical Powhatan Indian village of Maryland and Virginia, circa AD 1650

The intense storm having passed, I snuggled down between my soft, warm deerskin blankets and thanked the gods for making the winds and rain slow down. I could tell that Bright Light God had climbed above Big Water and was maybe halfway up the trees. Everyone else in my home was sound asleep. The flapping was getting softer. The strong wind blowing all night had loosened the vines that had been holding the door tightly shut. I mused along and guessed about what the powerful winds and heavy rains had done to Mother Earth. Curiosity finally forced me to get up, go quietly to the partially opened door, and peek outside.

Oooh! Aaah! Big trees had been broken off! Little trees were leaning almost flat. All were twisted and matted together. Little Water usually was farther away than I can throw a stone. Now it was a couple of steps from the hut. I could hear Big Water, an arrowshot away, roaring and crashing against the white sand.

What would the shoreline look like after such a powerful storm?

Quickly tying my hunting pouch (made from muskrat hides) around my waist, I took dried corn, beans, and fresh squash (to us, the Three Sisters of Life) from the containers, then took some more for my companion, and put the food in my pack. Trying to not arouse others, I quietly slipped out the door and headed toward my closest and best friend.

He is a slender, peeled, hickory stick that is about my height. Father gave me this friend four hot seasons ago after my ninth cold season. I named the stick Mucklik, which means "strong and quick." This stick and I are inseparable friends, the keenest of hunters, and the bravest warriors when we fight mock battles against wild savage animals (clusters of weeds or small bushes).

Of course, Mucklik is used to kill rabbits, opossums, snakes, birds, and other small animals. Sometimes I throw it like a spear, especially if the target is still. At other times, I sling it side-armed, making it twirl as it skims above the ground or water when the animal is moving. Then it hits like a club.

Mucklik and I are the truest of friends. I freely share secrets with Mucklik and tell him of the successes, accomplishments, worries, and trials—some real and some only imagined—that young braves face.

With Mucklik in hand, our scouting party began. I told him in my stern voice, or as sternly as I could make my voice sound, "Mucklik, good people must be respectful of all the good gods and make certain we do nothing that will make any god angry. Braves like us must always show courage when faced with dangers, and never—no, never lie to an elder brave or any good god. Strong braves [I placed emphasis on "strong," hoping to convince both of us that we are strong] always do right because it is always right to always do right, and only because it is always right to always do right! No other reason is needed or desired! Do you agree, my brave brother?"

Mucklik took all this in and kept silent. Silence indicates agreement, especially to strong, brave, young Indian warriors, as are the both of us—at least as I see things.

As we reached the beach, we stopped in amazement. The destruction and rubbish were beyond belief. Big Water was closer to the trees than I can ever remember. All the trees on the edge of the wooded area were broken off or blown down. Big mounds of sand were standing where it was level before. Even some trees inside the woods were blown down, and some were broken off at various heights above the ground.

It appeared that neither man nor beast could travel through such a tangled and mangled-up mess. It gave us an eerie feeling. We understand that this feeling comes from the spirits of the trees, saplings, vines, weeds, and grasses. Some, which were now dead, some were dying in misery, while others were in misery and getting better. Their spirits were calling out.

I knelt and asked Mucklik to pray with me to Big God. I then looked up and prayed out loud, "Dear most powerful God, who knows all things and can do all spiritual things, please give healing and comforting blessings to all who are hurting and weakened by Storm God."

A spirit of comfort came into me, making me believe that Big God had heard the prayer and that it would be done. My companion and I continued the patrol.

The scene was much different than what I was used to. The roots of the large downed trees stuck up in fascinating patterns. Some seemed to be a person's arms and legs sprawled out in every which way. Other roots reminded me of a woman's wet hair, frayed all around her head. Some looked like many large, hairy arms hanging over to grasp some unsuspecting animal or even stout braves, such as us! Yes! Braves must be vigil and extra careful when hunting in strange territory. This is no normal situation. A very powerful Goddess and God had just shown what they are able to do when they are angry. It is best that we advance using the highest caution.

There! See that movement in that big pine treetop lying on its side? Mucklik, that may be a very fierce enemy who has come to steal my older sister or, worse yet, capture Mother! We must move quietly and slowly and sneak up on him and send him to the Silent Hole, where he can never leave.

Upon getting close to that ghostly treetop, I lowered myself down and began to crawl very quietly toward our target. Bright Light God was now showing his full bright face. Sweat drops popped up on the smooth tan skin of my forehead. Nothing will stop a good warrior from getting to the enemy and killing him. Not heat, hunger, gnats, or mosquitoes. Thick and tangled brush may slow the progress, but warriors stop for nothing.

Finally, the assault position was reached. We sprang forward in full attack, yelling and screaming.

My friend was my weapon. I swung at and poked every bough and green pinecone I could reach on that tree. I then jumped up on the trunk, dashed to the upturned clump of roots. At the end of a high leap, I landed, standing on the very top of the upturned roots.

"Oohaah ooiee!" The warrior's victory cry rang out, loud and clear.

I looked at Mucklik and loudly proclaimed, "We are the strongest warriors in all this land. Nothing can stand against us!"

That said, I jumped down and headed out to the beach. Big Water was easing back away from the tree line, leaving trash of every nature strewn along in a continuous line. In one pile we found a dead fish, in another an odd-shaped limb. Some objects I have never seen before and had no idea of what they were. We inspected the line of rubble and trash for a long, long distance. Bright Light God was beaming down in full force. We slipped into the tree line to get in the shade.

Walking in the woods was slow going, but we were in no hurry. I remembered that on Little Water side of the woods one could find small streams of fresh water. We forced our way through the tangles to the far side of the trees. Walking outside of the tree line and just inside the edge of the marsh grass was easy walking. We made good time. I believed we would soon find fresh water.

Looking ahead, I noticed, as we rounded a curve in the wood line, that the woods became narrow about two arrow shots ahead. It appeared to be a likely place to find fresh, clear water. Being hot, thirsty, and hungry, I picked up the pace. Upon arriving at the spot where the woods were very narrow, I found the welcomed little stream, dropped to my stomach, and took a long, soothing drink. Sitting up in the cool shade, I took some food from my pouch and enjoyed a nice meal. Being full and cool, I leaned back, and was soon sound asleep.

The heat from Bright Light God, who had passed the treetops, caused me to arouse. The long trek and all the excitement had taken their toll. I noticed stiffness in my legs as I came fully awake. Mucklik was lying under them. Wind God had left. It was quiet. All seemed to be pleasant. I soaked up the scenery.

As I slowly turned my head, looking toward Big Water, I noticed a very slight movement in the tall grass that was close to the far side of the woods. I fixed my sight on that spot. Nothing. Yet I knew I had seen something move. Maybe a slight breeze had moved a leaf. Oh! There. It moved again! But it made just a little movement and stopped. I had no clue as to what it might be.

Had we been discovered by a raiding party of those feared Susquahannock people of the cold earth? They lived two Pale-Face Lights (two full moons) of walking away where it gets very cold. I learned of them from the stories told by the grown braves and the elders. Mother's sister had been captured by them and taken away. They were a large tribe. There was no way to get her back. What I saw could be a lead scout of a raiding party who had discovered us while I was sleeping.

I spoke to Mucklik, while holding him firmly in my grip, "Brother

Warrior, do not be afraid. We cannot show that we know he is there. Show no fear! We will sit here and make a plan, as though nothing is wrong. If we run, he will surely catch us."

I fixed my eyes on the spot. Every once in a while, the movement recurred, at irregular intervals. It always occurred in the very same location. Maybe it was a rabbit sitting there nibbling on the lush grass. Squirrels would not stay in one place. Yes! It must be a very wise enemy who keeps us in sight while waiting for the rest of his raiding party. That is a feather on his head that moves when he turns his head or when he brushes away the flies and gnats.

Now I can see something red and kind of flat just past the first movement. The red flat movement moves very slightly and slowly up and down. It is impossible to see but a little spot of it through the tall, thick grass.

"Mucklik, we have more than one enemy looking at us. Should we make a quick break and run with all our might to get away?"

"No. We do not know exactly what or who it may be. If we run and it is nothing but some plant or small animal, we will be embarrassed when others learn that we ran from nothing. We must move closer, learn exactly what it is, and then break away. That way, we will be honored as brave warriors who did what was right." I had answered my own question.

I slowly rolled onto my stomach and began to slowly and quietly crawl toward the spot. I never took my eyes from that area. I inched my way silently along. Father had taught me well on how to walk and crawl quietly. It took patience, willpower, and strong arms and legs. I continued to crawl until I could almost reach out with the stick and touch whatever it was that was moving. I slowly pushed my upper body up so I could get a good look through the tall grasses. It was not a rabbit's ear but the ear of a deer, for sure, and it was the funniest-shaped ear I had ever seen.

Then I realized that it was a large spotted animal, lying on its side, sound asleep with its red side moving up and down as it breathed. It was nothing I had ever heard of or seen! Its legs looked like posts, and its feet reminded me of a turtle with no legs. I remained propped up on my arms until they ached and trembled.

What was this thing I see? I must report it to the braves. This must be kept secret so as to not frighten the children and squaws. This is a serious thing! Maybe Storm God, in his fury, brought this to us. That means this thing may be very evil and can easily kill us. We must retreat and get back to our village.

I slowly moved Mucklit up so I could hold him in both hands, in case this thing awoke and charged. My plan was to slowly stand, leave quietly and quickly while the animal slept.

As I rose to stand, Sun God sent a shadow from my body over the sleeping thing. It raised its head! We both froze. A long stare at each other followed. What kind of alien is this? I pondered. The animal's eyes were soft as she soliloquized, "The young two-legs-no-feathers had a pleasant odor about him."

I quickly reasoned: if we ran, we would be caught, if the thing was an evil one. It seemed to have a peaceful spirit. I held my ground, as a brave warrior must.

The animal slowly placed the two front feet out to its front. That caught my eye. The animal slowly rose to all fours. I have never seen such an animal. It was much different than brother and sister deer.

I whispered to Mucklik, "It does not look like deer, and it rose from lying down by raising its front end first. Deer raise their back end first, and they make quick, sharp movements, as they get away, like a flash of lightning. This thing just stood there looking at us."

Smelling the savory food in his pouch, the paint filly stretched out her neck and nuzzled at the cover. She seemed harmless and hungry, so I opened the pouch and offered a handful of corn and beans. The animal nibbled the food and reached for more. That was repeated until all the food was gone. By that time, she was standing beside me.

I scratched her neck and back. Her hair was soft. She was thin but so gentle and friendly. I named her Bakting because she was calm and so friendly. She was a sister, much like sister deer. Bright Light God was creeping close to Little Water.

Pale-Face Light God was already showing overhead. Soon it would be dark. By getting on the beach, it would be a rather straight line to the hut. I headed for home. As I reached the beach I turned and looked back to see Bakting looking at us as if saying, "Don't leave." I quickly turned and left in jog. How am I going to explain finding this alien to my family? I did not know what it was, but I knew it was my friend. If Father or the braves learned of it, they would kill it to eat and keep the hide! No. I shall never betray my special friend. "Mucklit, we must keep this as our very own secret, forever."

As I neared our hut, I heard Mother's frantic calls. I answered by calling out, "I am coming," and quickly added, hoping she'd not ask, "Where have you been?", "I am so hungry I can eat a bear!"

I heard Mother laugh as she called back, "I have fish, oysters, raccoon, and cherries waiting!"

The hut was a welcome sight. The smell of the food added to the joy of being home again.

Secrets are hard to keep, especially for a young brave or maid. I shall not, must not ever share my secret about Bakting. Not to Sister, not to Mother, and especially not to any brave or to Father, for once he or any brave learns of her being on this island, Bakting will surely die! This secret must be kept, forever and ever!

With no questions being asked, the alien was safe. All is well.

Chapter 3

A WORLD OF SPIRITS

Oh, Mucklit, I am in a terrible mess. I must go see Bakting again! I am not even certain myself if I am merely dreaming a most wonderful dream or if I have discovered a new animal. Please tell me, Big God, why have I told so many tales that were made-up lies? I thought Mother or Father would like me more or believe that I am smart. How dumb can one brave warrior be? I am sure Mother knows most of the time when I am lying, as she often shoots me her "That sounds odd" look, and sometimes would get in, "If you lie, you have to have a good memory, or you'll have to lie to get out of a lie."

Mother is wise, as that is a fact. Lying is like trying to get free of being stuck in the stinking marsh mud by trying to go farther into the mudhole. Smart braves stay on the solid tussocks of grass and avoid the mucky holes.

Yes! That's what lies are. Stinky, sticky mudholes of the mouth! I'd love to go see my alien friend again today, but if I went off again so soon, I might have to lie to keep from being caught. Better yet, I am strong enough and smart enough to stop lying. Best I wait a day or two then leave early and get back before any questions about where I have been.

Fortunately, the harvest powwow was only a couple of Bright Lights away, and Father had plenty of work for me to do. The Assateague, Pocomoke, Wicomico, Nanticoke, and Choptank tribes come together in Big Woods to give thanks to and to honor Big God for Him providing ample food and shelter so people could live through the three or four moons of bitter cold.

Those who lived in Big Woods, beyond Little Water, acted like they were closer to Big God than us who lived on the Island. Mother was raised in Big Woods. She liked being on the island because we do not clear away sister and brother bushes and trees (they want to live too). We do not dig up Mother Earth to plant food, and then work three or four Pale-Face Lights of heat trying to kill the bugs and keeping brother and sister rabbit, raccoon, opossum, bear, and deer away.

Our squaws and maidens pick berries, cherries, persimmons, plums, and muscadines. They also dig up the needed roots. The braves hunt and fish. Big God is just as good to us as to those in Big Woods. "Some fail to understand other's ways," the elders claim. Mother also told us that those in Big Woods call us "Fish Heads" because we often smelled like smoked fish. Father claimed that it was not bad that they believed different than us. He says, "We all have to get along with each other to dodge the Silent Hole, from which no one ever returns."

Father told me that he needed help to finish burning out the big popular log to make a new canoe. He wanted it finished in time to cross Little Water on our way to the powwow. Our family had already given thanks to Brother Popular Tree for giving up his tree spirit. Upon Big God helping us finish making a canoe from the log, He would then give the log a good Canoe Spirit, if we looked for and did only the right things as Big God prefers. That made me wonder about spirits and gods.

I asked Father, "Why are there gods, spirits, and brothers and sisters that are not our kind?"

He taught me that gods have power to help, harm, and to change things and can affect people, animals, plants, and things around us. All things have a spirit. Big God has power over all gods and all things. Some things He controls by His rules, and some things He lets happen for many reasons, some reasons we never learn. Big God has some rules that cannot be broken by Him or by people or by anything, such as mothers can birth us only one time. When things get hot enough, they will be eaten by fire. Another is that birds can fly but people and many other animals cannot fly. Most of all, people and all other things can only be what we and they are: people, animals, or things. The deer cannot become a muskrat, and we cannot become a bear, or a cherry cannot become a squash.

On the other hand, there is nothing, spiritually, that Big God cannot do. People can have a mean spirit or a spirit to steal, lie, and cheat. Big God is able to change a bad spirit, especially, when asked. Big God can bring a new spirit to be born. Spirits are given only by Big God, but He allows us to grow our spirit as we choose. You make your spirit good or evil. The canoe will make its spirit. Maybe it will let water in or swim slowly and be known to have a weak or bad spirit. If it keeps water out and moves swiftly across the water, it will have a good spirit. As all of us will, the canoe will have a good or a bad spirit. Big God lets you shape and make your spirit much like shaping a canoe: burn out the bad parts and chip away what is not wanted.

Once Big God breathes life into a papoose, it becomes a living brave or maid. Each rock, tree, and even all non-breathing things have their own spirit. Being from Mother Earth, a rock gets the spirit of that rock. When we are born, Big God breathes a spirit into us. Then we become people. Before that breath from Big God, we are a part of our mother and her spirit, just as her leg is a part of her. We have our own spirit until it flies away to go where it should. Our body will go into the Silent Hole, to never return!

We must choose if our spirit is to be good. Once a body begins going into the Silent Hole, the good spirits float above with the Bright Light God, Pale-Face Light God, Big God, and the many fires of the night sky. There your spirit will remain happy and warm forever. Nothing changes about a spirit once the spirit leaves our body. Bad spirits must go into the dark, silent hole to never be happy again.

Look at a turkey egg. It is an egg until it gets the spirit of life, then it becomes a living turkey and it begins to shape its spirit. A spirit may stay with its body a very short time, no longer than it takes you to wiggle a toe, or the spirit may stay with its body for many Pale-Face Lights. Study the acorn. When does it become a tree and stop being a nut that we grind, cook, and eat? The acorn stops being a nut when it cracks out of its shell, when it gets its own spirit of life, and then begins living as an oak tree. It will have its very own spirit as an oak. It cannot be any other kind of tree, and it will be known as an oak tree until it gives up its spirit as a tree. Then it may become an oak post, wood for fire, or it may rot.

We are people as long as we have a spirit, which is given by Big God. If brother or sister turkey had no spirit, it would always act exactly as its brothers and sisters. They would act exactly alike, if there was no turkey spirit. If an oak tree had no spirit, it would look and act as do all other oaks. They would all break at the same places, have knots at the same places, all would give the same number of nuts for us to eat, and all would fall in the same storm if there were no oak tree spirit. If we had no spirit, we would behave exactly as all our brothers and sisters. Spirits are known by how things, animals, and people behave and act.

No two spirits are exactly alike. Some are especially kind, some are mean, most are good. We have sisters and brothers of many kinds who live with or among us, as friends. They help us live. We call animals and some things Mother, Father, Brother, and Sister out of respect for them and how they live and help us live. Respect all things, even those that can and will harm you.

"Love people. Use things! Never switch them around," the wise ones teach us.

Father ended talking by claiming, "Gods—such as Bright Light God, Storm God, Thunder God, and Lightning God, and some others—are powerful. They too have a spirit. They do not live among people and are not a part of people. They are powerful. Why they are here, we do not know. We do know some of their ways."

Father is wise. Working with and learning from Father brings a warm, pleasant feeling deep in my chest.

Making a canoe is hard, slow work. Burning and then chipping out the burned parts with handheld stones makes your fingers sore and brings pains to your arms and back. First, we burned the outside parts that we do not want or need. Once burned deep enough, we chipped the burned parts away until the shape of the outside is as Father wants, curved and smooth.

Father wants this canoe to be shaped similar to a big bean pod. The outside bottom will be curved slightly upward on both ends (that's why Father chose a tree with a slight curve in its trunk), and both ends will be shaped like the point of an arrow. Then we burned the inside and chipped away the burned parts, until the fire had burned as close to the sides, ends, and bottom as Father wanted.

While the fire burned, we caught some fish and crabs to eat before going to sleep. The day passed quickly. We did not finish making the canoe. I knew what I'd be doing the next day, making and keeping the fires going and chipping with a large oyster shell. The next day, while the fire burned in the canoe, we caught more fish and smoked them over hickory wood. The smoke keeps the flies and bugs away, keeps the meat from rotting, and makes the meat taste the very best. We had a good day!

Chapter 4

AN ISLAND CHANGED

The fire at the village circle was burning bright that evening as we approached. Every brave, it seemed, of our village was there. The two elder chiefs who had the most powerful spirits of any in our village were there. One was a stern Medicine Man who knew and understood more than any other in our village. He talked and visited with spirits. His spirit was powerful and comforting. The other elder was the bravest and strongest warrior in our village. His courage and strength were held in high respect not only in our village, and he was admired by all who knew him. His feats in hunting and in war were often told in great detail around other village fires. When total strangers visited us and during the big powwow in the Big Forest, even strangers knew him or knew of some of his daring feats. There was a festive air about the coming powwow as it grew dark.

This is an important meeting because everyone, including squaws and children, were invited. There will be no talk of war, enemy raids, nor raids by us Assateague people tonight. I knew that because the squaws and the very young were present. Every grown brave made a formal greeting to each elder chief. Then some friendly exchanges were made between and about the braves.

As the fire died down, the wise chief stood and faced the gathering.

All movement and talking stopped. The squaws and the children who had formed behind the men made not one whisper or a whimper.

The Medicine Chief began. "Good people of the great Assateague tribe, please join me in praise and thanks to Big God."

With that, he lifted both arms, looked skyward, and only as a devout person can, he talked to Big God. Upon lowering his arms, he continued, "My people, we have heard for many hot seasons [summers] stories of strange, Pale-Face people coming from far across Big Water. They visit our warm lands that are many Pale-Face Lights of walking or paddling a canoe from here. It takes a warm season of Pale-Face lights walking to get to those places.

"Before the Pale-Faces came, there are stories that many, many Pale-Face Lights ago, some Pale-Faced people, with hair on their faces the color of blood, visited our cold white-feather-hard-water [snow] land. The blood-faced came to a place about one Pale-Face Light of walking from here. Why any of them come to our land, we do not know. From where they come, we do not know.

"The Pale-Faces who visit the warm land tries always to explain that there is only one God and that He knows and can do everything. They say He is everywhere at one time as is light, when Bright Light God is seen, and as is dark, when Bright Light God is hiding. We Assateagues, our brothers and our sisters, know their god cannot do everything because when a Paleface is asked, 'Can your one god make a rock so big he cannot pick it up?' the paleface has no reply. We who know spirits know that spiritually, Big God can do anything that is spiritual.

"Some physical things are impossible, even for the gods. Neither man nor beast can ever return the baby to the inside of the mother and both live, but spiritually, we can be born again—when we accept a new way of living.

"Pale-Faces, we are told, have strange animals. Something bigger than deer. They ride on them and place pouches on them loaded with whatever they bargain for or take. A wise brother Medicine Man came to us many hot seasons [summers] ago by walking two hot seasons. His people are Pueblo who understand Sister Corn better than all others. Sister Rain does not often visit them. They make streams from the running waters to their patches of corn so the three sisters may drink.

"The Pueblo Medicine Man told us that the big, strong animals which the Comanche people sit on are called cayuse. People with pale faces, as is the Pale Light God, came to Comanche country many, many cold seasons ago and left cayuses. It is known that when Pale-Faces leave a village, they take all the gold, silver, gems, and blankets they can get. They take some of our plants that we eat, we are told by our brother Medicine Man. Also, we know when the Pale-Faces leave, they leave sickness, contention, and anger in the villages they visited. Many Pale-Faces have a hard spirit.

We Assateagues, Pocomokes, Wicomico, Nanticokes, and Choptank people have been protected from Pale-Faces by Big God. We give Him our thanks!"

He continued, "Today some of our braves found on the white sand beside Big Water many strange poles and logs that must be the remains of the big canoe the Pale-Faces make. The braves found them because the birds that eat animals that have lost their spirits to never return, were feasting on animals the medicine man painted as a cayuse. None of us had ever seen a cayuse. I am certain that the animals being devoured by the birds are cayuse. They had no spirit because they had gone into the Silent Hole to never return. "Many cayuses were under and among the poles, logs, and big robes that lie on the sand. Maybe Storm God broke the canoe and took the spirits of the cayuse and of the Pale-Faces. No Pale-Face was in the pile. We people of this land must be prepared to see Pale-Faces here before many more hot seasons. I believe they will come. We must welcome them. Try to teach them a better way. "Pale-Faces do not know the gods we know. Pale-Faces do not feel the spirits we feel. We must help them to be brothers and sisters with the many spirits we know. Then all can live in peace and be happy, be friends."

The meeting was over.

I am certain that Bakting is a cayuse.

Chapter 5

FINDING BAKTING

As Sun God began to come up and peek over Big Water, Tangtok placed as many of the Three Sisters (beans, squash, and corn) into his muskrat pouch as he guessed he could take without raising any questions from Mother about the amount. With Mucklit in hand, he stepped out in a brisk walk, heading toward the beach. With Sun God on his left and the pocosin woods on his right, he made a beeline toward where he last saw Bakting.

The woods were littered with dead limbs and broken-off treetops. Many of the young trees were still bent from the force of Storm God, and some had stood up to almost as they were before the big winds. Maybe young trees were smart enough to bend with the wind that was stronger than the trees, while the big old trees were too hard-headed to bend their ways, so the powerful Storm God broke them in two to show that it is sometimes best to get along and keep your spirit, as Dad told me earlier.

Big Water was rolling gently onto the white sand. Shore birds were scurrying along and then springing into the air to fly a little way, land, peck at some tasty morsel, and fly again. Fluffy balls of clouds were slowly drifting along. What a great feeling it is to be walking along with your very best friend, smelling Big Water, the pine boughs, and the tangy bushes. Big God is just so good to people! He proves that He loves us by all the good things He does for us every day.

Soon I arrived at place where I first met Bakting. I visited the spring head and searched along the streamlet as it trickled toward the marsh along the edge of Little Water. There was no sign of the alien.

"Mucklit, where do you think she may be?"

A careful search up and down then across the marsh grasses offered no hint of his animal friend. She must be farther toward the far end of our island close to where the Chincoteague people live.

"We must move on, Mucklit."

Moving along the edge of the marsh and next to the trees was much harder travelling than walking along the beach, but the best chance of seeing any tracks or other sign—such as twigs being bent, scat on the ground, and grasses being bitten off—was between the pocosin area and the tidal marsh. Most animals, such as the deer, bobcats, and raccoons, bedded down in the woods and moved out into the marsh to feed. Bakting most likely did likewise.

Time was slipping away, and no sign was found. Where could the animal be? After travelling as long and as fast as we have, I must be very careful as my dad, other braves, and the elders often mentioned when sitting around the village fire at nights, "If any evil people came to the island, they usually came to this part where no one lived, and very few came to hunt animals or to gather food." I will move more quietly and check for any sign of people having travelled this way.

Bright Light God was a little past directly overhead. It was hot, with little to no breeze. Still, there was no sign of man or Bakting. Up ahead, there appeared an exceptionally large copse of trees that formed a very long point into Little Water. If I find nothing between here and there, I must turn back, or my family will be too curious about where I have been. Being excited, the pace increased to a slow jog at times where the ground was solid. The copse of trees was too thick with bushes, brush, and vines for any large animal to penetrate, and there was very little grass for food or a bed. Farther out toward the point, the trees spread out, and the undergrowth was much thinner. That is most likely where a big animal would seek refuge.

The marsh grass made it impossible to see clearly what may be under those trees. It looked like a good place for an animal to be. Anxious to investigate out to the end of the point, I shifted from a jog to a trot. I just knew and felt in my chest that Bakting was close! My attention was fixed ahead as I pressed on.

"Stop!" I heard a strange voice.

What was that? I squatted down and slowly turned my head toward the woods from where the sound came. *Uhuhuh*—a soft, guttural voice. There it is again, in the woods. I stretched up a little and spied a slight movement. Then I saw that big ear, which I remember so well.

Immediately I stood up. I could not believe my eyes! There stood Bakting and several more of her kind just behind her! They were easing away from her and me. That let the bolt of fear that jolted me to quickly slip away. Bakting eased toward me with her nose stretched out testing the air. She knew I had food. Maybe she smelled the food before she heard or smelled me.

As I pulled a handful of food from my pouch, her muzzle reached my hand. I flattened my hand, palm up, as she nibbled vigorously. The other animals stopped, turned their heads as if to say, "What is that dumb thing doing fooling around with a Two-legs-no-feathers? Doesn't she know that some of them are evil?"

As Bakting continued to eat, I told her about the canoe and what we had been doing. I asked her about the other animals. She made no response to my curiosity. At least she was no longer alone. I noticed that two of her kind are squaws like her, and one was a brave, such as brother deer. One of the squaws had the kindest look in her eyes. She was the first to move up beside Bakting. I offered her a handful of food. She had the softest muzzle, almost as soft as milkweed feathers. She had a very gentle spirit, much as Bakting's spirit.

The brave held his head up high, tossing it up and down as though he was annoyed by all this. He had a hard, mean look in his eyes, with a solid, white ring around the outside of them. Every once in a while, he would gently paw the ground and shake his head sideways, as if to say, "Let's get out of here! Ole two-legs-no-feathers has nothing we want or need!"

The squaw ate until the food was gone, paying little to no attention to his commotion. Knowing that Bakting had more of her kind to be with made a pleasant feeling settle over me. She now has her own kind. I thanked Big God.

I made it back to the hut just as Bright Light God began to slip behind the trees on the far side of Little Water. Mother had stewed squash, hominy, fresh roasted muskrat, and cool muscadines to eat, under the brush arbor. When we finished eating, Father said he was going to the village circle to hear what the other braves had to talk about.

Chapter 6

ANNUAL POWWOW

The Big Powwow was the only thing, lately, that our village people talked about. It would start two more Bright Lights away. It will last until people stop coming and the food is gone. Some from our village were already crossing Little Water in their canoes. My family, as other families, had prepared many baskets of dried deer, turkey, raccoon, rabbit, musk-rat, fish, and fresh plants, berries, and roots. We loaded our new canoe. Father and Big Sister paddled the new canoe. Mother and I were in my canoe. Father gave me the old canoe for working so hard on the new one. Mother said she could not tell who was the happiest with their canoe, Father or me. As soon as Bright Light God had hidden, we slept.

When Bright Light God began chasing away the dark, we began paddling toward the far side of Little Water. We were excited about our new canoes and clothes. We were anxious to show our new shoes, leggings, and fur capes. When Bright Light God showed His full face, the warm clothes were opened or laid aside. We began singing songs as we paddled along. One of Father's favorites that his father taught him was this:

> Brother Squirrel has a bushy tail.
> Brother Possum's tail is bare.
> Brother Rabbit has no tail at all,
> Just a little bunch of hair!
> The raccoon up the tree.
> The opossum in the hollow.
> The raccoon dropped a grape.
> The opossum got a swallow.[6]

Singing made paddling much easier.

We banked our canoes in a quiet cove with a sandy shore that was shaded by big oak trees. The ground was covered with canoes. I did not know that there were so many canoes on Mother Earth. None were as pretty and strong as ours. We tied our bundles of food under two poles. Mother and Father carried one pole between them with the biggest load slung under it. They wrapped part of a beaver hide around the ends of the pole for padding and placed one end of the pole on one of their shoulders, Father in front. Big Sister and I carried the lighter load with a padded pole on our shoulders. I was in front.

Father said we would be halfway to the powwow camp when Bright Light God slid under Mother Earth. Five fingers of rest stops later, we camped until Bright Light God returned.

Just before Bright Light God showed his face, we were on the trail again. We reached the moving sweet water of the Pocomoke people as Bright Light God began slipping behind the trees. We hastily built brush huts, with sleeping mounds inside. Many huts were scattered through the forest as far as one could see. There were clusters of huts on both sides of the sweet running water. Several fires were burning. The smell of roasted meat was everywhere.

Father and Mother quickly began talking and laughing with many different people. Some I remember from the last powwow. Some I had never seen before. As Bright Light God slid behind the treetops, Father and I cut and gathered brush and limbs while Mother and Sister made sleeping mounds. By dark, we had a cozy place to sleep. Our campfire was burning between us and the running water.

Several young people my age came to visit and help as dark closed in around us. With Pale-Face Light God being big and bright and the fires burning, it was as if Bright Light God was above us. We had races out into the forest and back. We threw rocks at knots in the trees and tried to see who could throw a rock over the top of a big, tall gum tree. We ate every kind of food there was until we hurt. We could hear the braves shouting and laughing over by the village fire. Parents began calling to their families to come and be quiet.

The noise muffled down until all was quiet. We crawled onto our sleeping mounds. The frogs and crickets sang their songs in the dark. Father thanked Big God.

Bright Light God's warm face aroused me from a deep sleep. I heard some young people playing in the sweet running water. Immediately I headed that way in a brisk run. The running water was filled along each side with young braves, maidens, old braves, squaws, and the elders. Some were swimming, some were tussling with each other, and some we shouting to others on the far side.

I dove into the clear, cool water and swam a long way underwater. I came up a little father out than most of them on my side of the water. I was very close to those on the far side.

While those on the far side appeared to have many of our features, I was surprised that their faces and hair were different than ours. I could hear them talking, and understood some of what they were saying. I could not understand most of what they said. Some on our side did understand them as they were talking back and forth with no difficulty. As I swam around, some of the young braves I had met swam out to me.

We picked out a tree on our shoreline that was about an arrow shot away, and all agreed to race to the tree. We agreed that when one of the blackbirds flying over landed on the marsh grass we would start. I watched closely. As one bird flared to land, I took a big gulp of air. When its feet touched the blade of grass, I kicked forward and paddled with my arms as fast as I could.

I kept my head down, stroked with my arms outstretched and as fast as possible until I had no breath left. Quickly, I turned my face up, gulped air between strokes, and kept kicking and stroking. It was kick-stroke-kick-stroke-kick-stroke-gulp air and back to the kick-stroke rhythm. I could tell one other boy was close to me and no one was ahead of us. I stroked and kicked harder.

My strength was ebbing, but I kept up my rhythm. My arms got heavier with each stroke. I was dying for a deep breath of fresh air, but I had to show those Big Forest young bucks that I am better than they are. I kept stroking and kicking with all my might. As I gulped air, I saw the tree just past my fingers. On my next stroke, my other hand hit the tree. I grabbed the root sticking out and looked around. I was the only one at the tree. I thanked Big God that I had often swam in Big Water even when the water rolled high over my head. My newfound friend was the first to reach me. We both were gasping for air and sounded like Mother Bear huffing at her cubs. The tree we were holding on to was at a narrow part of running water. I heard voices on the far side. I pulled myself up to get a better view.

Chapter 7

A FRIENDSHIP FLOURISHES

I saw three maidens: one younger, one older than me, and one about my age. They were sitting in half-circle, facing us, talking to each other and laughing, splashing water and giggling as silly maidens do. The middle-aged one was sitting the closest to us. She looked up. She was not a stone's throw away.

Our eyes met. I froze and shook all over at the very same time. I could not move or even blink my eyes. She was the most beautiful person I had ever seen. She reminded me of Mother. Her eyes were soft and clear. Her skin was smooth, the color of a wet hickory nut. Her hair was the color of sister Crow. Her nose and chin gave her a most charming appearance. I could not help but to notice the form of her chest. She was no child. I detected a slight smile as she slowly lowered her head and turned her gaze back toward the far bank.

I almost slipped under the water before I caught myself. A feeling started in my chest. The warm, fuzzy feeling went down and up at the same time. That was making me feel weak and warm at the same time. What kind of spirit did that maid have? She made this strong, young brave tremble all over.

I felt as though I were standing in the middle of a big village fire and all eyes were on me! I started to call out to her. Words did not come. Oh, well, she is of another tribe. I do not know her language. I would not be able to make her understand me, anyway.

Noticing that I was staring at the maids across the water, my friend told me, "Those are sisters. They are daughters of the great warrior chief of the Choptank people. He is one of the most respected chiefs within our tribes. He has fought many battles against the raiding and hunting parties of the Susquehannock and Cold Country people."

My mind raced. I care not about her father or her mother! I must find a way to see her. I will find a way. I scampered up the near bank, heading to speak with Father. As I turned around and looked back, the three maids were up and running away.

I ran to my family's hut. I was hungry. Most of all, I had some very important business to discuss with Father. While sitting and eating, I asked him, "Why is it that no one swims across the river to visit those on the far side?"

Father explained, "It was not proper for our people, especially the warriors or braves, to cross the river until their High Chief of the Choptank tribe is present. He is the highest chief of all. Our people do not enter his lands until he invites us.

"In the past, a few of our braves have taken maids from their villages without the chief's or the family's approval. This made bad medicine. Their High Chief, many of his braves, and some of the Nanticoke braves have not returned from a trading and hunting party. Father said he heard that the High Chief is only two or three Bright Lights away. Once he arrives, all chiefs will meet with him and his chiefs. He will then make known the families who have available maids, what games will be played, and the rules that must be followed during visits and during the games. Then all can visit any of the others, and the games will begin."

I asked, "If one were to cross the river before the High Chief returns and gets caught over there, what would happen?"

Father's reply came as a stern warning. "Breaking a rule brings big trouble. One who breaks this rule must run the gauntlet. The gauntlet is two lines of their braves, two arms lengths apart with a stick in one hand. The rule breaker—brave or maid—must hop or crawl, with legs tied loosely together, between the lines. The bad one is beaten with sticks as they hop along. Some never finish before they go to the Silent Hole. The Silent Hole may be the best thing. A brave or maid being disgraced before all villages will be treated forever worse than a liar or a thief."

The day was passing slowly. I did enjoy meeting many of the young people my age from the other tribes who remained on our side of the running water. We played games, had several races, and shot arrows at targets. The games were new to me, but I learned them quickly. I was one of the fastest runners and won most of the races. Only a couple young braves came close to shooting an arrow as far as I could. I beat all of them shooting small squash in the dead center.

Then, I hung a pinecone from a limb using a vine. I asked one friend to stand behind the tree and, by using a long stick, make the cone swing back and forth. I was the only one who hit the cone every time shooting three arrows. One of the Chincoteague maids became my staunchest supporter. She brought me cool water in a gourd from the spring. She always ran to pick up my arrows before others could. She was strong and very fast. She always beat the other maidens in their games. She gained my attention, that is for certain. I enjoyed her being around.

However, the Choptank maiden was constantly on my mind. *How long would it be before I saw her again? Would she be willing to talk to me?* Oh, how I longed for her to see me in the races or watching me shoot arrows. I wonder if she would care about another maiden bringing me water and arrows.

The hottest part of the day called us to the cool running river. Nothing could have suited me better. I ran, full speed, my heart was racing. I knew that the beautiful maiden would be on the far side of the river. I must learn her name! Oh, just to see her again!

My feet flew faster. I was bursting with energy. The pain in my side meant nothing. The rest of my friends were so far behind that I could not even hear their feet hitting the dry dirt. I reached the bank at full speed, took a long leap, and did my very best to get as far out as possible. The second my eyes broke the surface, I searched the far side. Many people of all ages were in the water. Too many little children were splashing and dashing about. Where was the maid with those bright eyes and the most beautiful face? I saw her sisters sitting quietly in water that came up to their necks, but no bright-eyed maid. Where could she be?

My other playmates closed around me and starting tussling and splashing one another. I dove under and swam as far away as I could toward the tree where the race had ended the day before. After surfacing I quietly paddled along. I was relieved to be alone. I was really angry but did not know why.

Eventually, I quietly reached the big tree and took hold of the same root I had grasped at the end of the race.

Chapter 8

RULES GET BROKEN

The quietness was comforting. I slowly rolled over. Holding on to the root, I let my mind wonder while slowly moving my legs as if walking. All my thinking was of the captivating maid. How tall was she? How many Cold Seasons had she seen? Was she funny or solemn? I know she can run fast by the build of her body above those slender, shapely legs. Her hair must flow straight back as the wind makes it wave up and down when she runs.

I decided to get up on the bank so I could scan the other side of the river. The big tree leaned out over the water, so I chose to stand on the leaning trunk, where I could get a clear view. There was a small branch pointing back toward the land that was just above my head. I stepped up on the trunk and reached up to grasp the limb when a slight movement in the water next to the tree caught my eye. I froze! Two of the most captivating eyes locked onto mine.

This must be a big mistake! My mind has tricked me! The face was the very same one that had been locked in my head since I last saw her. We both gasped as our breaths escaped us. She should not be here, as she surely will be severely punished or killed.

I leaped into the river to quickly hide her. There really was no way to hide her if anyone one on either side of the river happened to look at the right spot. I would not, could not accept that!

As I slipped into the water, our wet, warm bodies made full contact. When my feet landed on hers, my chest was just above hers. I never felt anything as soft and warm as her vibrant body. Her eyes were soft as a mother deer's. Her lips were firm and as beautiful as a rainbow.

My arms automatically cuddled her firmly against my body. My burning thought was that she must be hid and protected. This precious maiden was in serious trouble if anyone learned she was on this side of the river. We must act as quick as a rabbit.

We both were frozen motionless. One of her arms was over my shoulder, and the other arm was under my opposite arm. A ring of warm feelings flowed down around my entire body. She was dead still with her body slightly touching mine.

Everything went eerily quiet. No birds chirped. No leaves rustled. Nothing moved. I gently lifted her and cradled her in my arms, much as a squaw would a baby. She was as light as feather to me. I knew I must move much like brother fox, who slyly melts out of sight then dashes away. Move too fast and we will draw attention, like a bolt of lightning. Move too slow, and if anyone spied us, they would recognize who we were.

As stealthily as we could, we slowly eased, mostly submerged, upriver to where some low-lying limbs covered the bank. We silently melted into the thickest part of the woods. Coming upon a soft, mossy area covered with dark shade from large pin oaks, I gently placed my treasured load onto the comfortable bed of leaves.

Neither of us had spoken a word. As I sat down beside her, she turned toward me, wrapped her hands around my head, gently eased my head down, and pressed her pursed, warm lips against mine. My chest swelled with emotion. I lost contact with life as my mind exploded with thoughts, scenes, and visions. This was the most wonderful feeling I had ever experienced in my life. Certainly, Big God has His hand on all this!

As her head leaned back, her face burst into a captivating smile, with little dimples in each cheek. Touching the center of her chest with both hands, the smile still beaming, she said, "Meelowtiekee," and pointed to my chest with one hand. Her fingertip was soft and warm as a beam of sun.

Suddenly, I realized she was asking for my name. Being struck by her beauty and poise, I softly murmured, "Tangtok." She giggled, as maidens do, and nodded her head in approval of my name. With a wry smile, she let my name flow from her lips, "Taangteeok." She quickly made a fist and curled her right arm up to her shoulder, flexing her muscles to show she understood that my name meant "strong."

Time flew as we did our best to explain our names and to describe our families. I learned that her name meant "lightning-fast chipmunk," and she preferred being called Tiekee. Bright Light God was sinking behind the trees. We stood and warmly embraced each other. She took my hand and led me to the bank of the river. She turned, released my hand, and again placed both hands behind my head and gently pressed my lips against hers. Neither of us tried to pull away for the longest time. What a wonderful, warm feeling. This maid must have been sent by a very kind god!

Realizing that dusk was falling, I finally found the strength to ease back. I motioned toward the river. In a flash, she dove from the bank, slipped silently into the water, and was gone. She stayed under so long that I started to dive in to rescue her. Just as I took a step toward the river, her head silently slipped into view way beyond the center of the river. Silently she dog-paddled to the far shore. I could hardly see her slim, shapely body as she finally stood. She turned, waved ever so softly, and, with a couple of springing steps, disappeared into the woods above the far bank.

I felt that I had just waved goodbye to the best person on Mother Earth. My heart was pounding. An exhilarating feeling surged through my entire body. I believed that I could wrestle a grown bear to the ground and leap to the top of the tallest tree!

After savoring many different roasted meats and tasting several new mixtures of fruits and nuts, I found quiet solace in our hut. Sleep did not come. Tiekee learned that I lived on an island, but did she know that her people referred to my people as "Fish Heads"? What is going to happen to her if her family learns she crossed the river? And then learn why?

The most worrisome thing is this: what must I do to see her again? For certain, I cannot let anyone know we met.

The night was one of the longest in my life.

Chapter 9

THE GAMES BEGIN

As Bright Light God began warming Mother Earth, I made a visit to the huts that served the most delicious food. At the second hut I visited, several of my newfound friends came together. They were anxious to begin our fun and games. Several were sure they could now beat me shooting arrows. No one wanted to wrestle or race me. I believe they had spent the evening practicing while I was with Tiekee.

The first challenge was to learn who could shoot an arrow the farthest. We marked our arrows with our choice of colors made from fruits and herbs and began shooting. Each was allowed to shoot three arrows.

As the group headed to pick up and check whose arrows flew the longest distance, the Chincoteague maiden jogged up beside me. She flashed a bright smile as I acknowledged her joining me. Having not earlier learned her name, I told her mine and asked for hers. She replied that her father said she was as pretty as a blue heron, so that is what he named her, Cindakwah. He called her Dakwee—Baby Heron.

We had to go farther than the other shooters as two of my arrows were beyond all others. Dakwee told me about her family and that they lived across from the southern end of my Island on a big round island. It took them two Bright Lights of paddling their canoes to get to the cove where we grounded our canoe. Their village was two Bright Lights of hard walking from mine.

Upon returning to the camping site, we learned that High Chief Cohloka of the Choptanks had arrived and all the chiefs were now meeting with him. Everyone was to remain close to their fires. No swimming and no visiting until the meeting of the chiefs ended. Families and friends joined together around their fires where they usually met. Dakwee and I spent the rest of the Bright Light at the same fire. We learned much about each other.

During the conversations between the squaws and braves, it became clear that there had been bad medicine between our people and the Big Woods people. Our people were looked down upon by the Big Woods tribes. Their maids would sometime accept marrying our braves, but their braves hardly ever took one of our maids for a wife. The Big Woods braves and chiefs usually took squaws who were of the cold earth tribes.

My mother and father agreed with those who claimed that an Assateague brave would find it very difficult in gaining the hand of a maid from any of the Big Woods tribes. All agreed that no chief of the Big Woods tribes would ever accept their daughters marrying a "Fish Head." A roaring laugh burst out when one declared that no brave or warrior of the Big Woods would ever come asking for a Fish Head squaw. That would never happen. Big Woods people believed they were far better than Fish Heads.

My thoughts of seeing Tiekee again drifted farther and farther apart. The presence of Dakwee, with her friendly, wholesome ways, clouded the thoughts of the brazen Tiekee. In fact, Dakwee was becoming a lot more attractive, and several other young maidens seemed to be more charming and attractive.

When our chiefs returned, the games, the rules for, and where the games in which our tribes would compete were announced. There would be, by age groups, during the next two days: foot races, wrestling, and tomahawk throwing. The big event, on the third day, will be "Stick Ball," or "Little War," for the mature braves. The Medicine Men and some of the young chiefs would be coaches and referees. They often prayed over the participants, their tomahawks, sticks, and other possessions. Most importantly, they passed advice and guidance to the competitors.

Traditionally, the squaws, maidens, and the very young would provide food, refreshments, and medical aid during the events. I was selected to compete in the foot race, wrestling, and tomahawk throw against young bucks in my age group.

The powwow began in earnest that evening. The braves and maids danced, sang, chanted, ate, and enjoyed the fruit juices and drinks of cool spring water. A group of us young people—including Dakwee, who stayed close to me—went for a swim. I was on edge as I had no plan of what to do when Tiekee saw us two together.

Dakwee and I enjoyed swimming and tussling in the water until full dark. My concern was for nothing as Tiekee never came to the river, or if she did, I did not know it. I wondered what may have happened to her. Maybe she was in big trouble! I was disappointed in not seeing her. Yet at the same time, I was relieved that I did not have to face her while Dakwee was with me. Really, I was confused by my own feelings about all this and these two attractive maids who never left my mind.

Chapter 10

THE BIG RACE

The next day came early as many were up at daylight dancing, shouting, and chanting in preparation for the competitions. The Medicine Men were placing special marks, some with assorted colors, on members they were coaching. Everyone was in high spirits.

My father brought a Medicine Man Chief to me. Father told me the Medicine Man would be my coach and he would help me win the games I played in. As the Medicine Man placed war marks on me, he told me about the young braves who would be competing against me. He knew all of them. I was glad for his words, as I had not met any of the braves who were on the other side of the river.

I missed one moving target when throwing the tomahawk, but placed second out of ten young braves. I had to wrestle three different young braves. The third one was for the championship. It took all the skill and energy I had. My coach was the main reason I won the championship. He had been a longtime wrestling champion at many powwows. He knew exactly what moves for me to make, and his warnings saved me several times. There was no celebration of me being the wrestling champion, and my coach had failed to inform me of who my last opponent was, until later.

In private, he told me that I had defeated High Chief of the

Choptanks, Cohloka's son, and asked that I join him later at his hut. I was honored by our Medicine Chief's invitation. The Chief warmly welcomed me and asked that I say no more after our talk. I promised.

He had a look of concern on his wrinkled face as he shared, "You are a very special brave. Only you and I have ever defeated a Choptank in wrestling. I chose to not let you know who you had to wrestle for the championship as it may have clouded your thinking."

Oh no! I thought. *The chief knew about Tiekee and the river and me!* I remained still and tried to not show any sign or concern.

"You beat the Chief's youngest son, who is a twin of his oldest daughter, and that son is the pride of the Ole Warrior's heart. Had you known any of this and who your opponent was, it could have lessened your spirit to win."

Now, I know the Chief knows about us! I kept a blank face.

"No big celebration was held in hopes that no ill feelings would be kindled to a boiling point. Leaving some things undone is sometimes better to only thinking about doing another thing. Especially, in this case, since we just learned that High Chief Cohloka has restricted one daughter until Bright Light God is directly overhead, because she asked if he would approve of her visiting with several of the young maidens and braves of the Assateague people."

Realizing that no names had been made known, I quickly stood and solemnly confirmed that I agreed with the chief that "all is well that ends well."

He directed that I leave, and added, "You will be a great warrior who is needed in our tribe."

Bright Light God was well past overhead when six of us young braves, about my age, where told to report in full battle markings for the race. I was a little sore from the wrestling but felt rested and strong. My coach introduced us to each other. The other four were sons of lower or middle chiefs. When a brave was introduced, the others walked up to him, and in turn, we raised our hands, palm forward, and pressed our palms against his—the sign of friend.

Two of them were taller than me. One was my height. Two were shorter than me. We were instructed to run around a swamp that was a very long arrow shot in length and only half as wide. We had to stay outside of the trees marked with two notches. The other four had warrior braves as their coaches.

The oldest warrior stated the rules. The signal to start will be when a bird that he points out lands. If anyone jumps out early, we must not run. No runner may touch another at any time during the race. The notched trees must always be between the runners and the lake. The first one to jump over the big log lying at the finish line and have one foot on the ground is the winner. The winner receives a hunting hatchet. We were guided to the finish-line log. It was about as high as my hip. They then moved us over to where a warrior drew the start line in the dirt with a stick. They had us place one big toe on the line. There was one tall runner at the near end of the mark, then a short runner, then me, another short runner, and the other tall one on the far end. The warrior had us to move one double-arm's length apart. He pointed out a blue jay flying overhead toward our front, and told us when its feet touches a limb, to start.

We got into a good starting position as the bird flitted along. The bird set its wings, stretched out its feet to land, glided to a stop, and just as his feet touched the limb, we sprang out like Brother Rabbit does! The tall one to the outside of me and the short one inside of me eased out into the front of me after several strides. A large tree loomed directly to our front. The tall one went to the outside the short one took the inside, with me on his heels. Some large roots were showing above the ground close to the tree. I heard one behind me stumble.

The pace was so fast I thought I was not able to run this fast much longer or I will not be able to finish. The short one just in front of me eased out to the front. I eased up and ran beside the tall one. A patch of tall grass came into sight. The one up front did not slow down. He hit the patch at top speed. The tall one beside me was directly behind the leader. I slowed just little to ensure I did not trip.

About two-thirds across the grassy patch, the lead runner did stumble just a little. Both he and the tall one dropped back behind me. I eased up my pace, and soon, they were beside me. I held my pace. They did not pass me. We dodged several more trees. A marshy area was just ahead. Obviously, the stream leading from the lake was coming up. Initially, we could find hard spots to step on while making good time. Then the solid spots disappeared. Nothing but ankle-deep mud.

I stopped running on my toes and made sure I placed my feet down, flat-footed. I didn't sink as far as if I had kept my toes pointed down, and I had more spring in the mud. I was in the lead when I crossed the stream bed. The soft mud stretched out a little farther on the far side. I eased up and let them get up beside me. I caught my second wind just as I hit solid ground. One runner was way behind us. The other two sprinted out ahead. I let them get about two full steps ahead before I, too, picked up the pace.

Then came another tree. They both went to the inside and hit a soft spot. I went to outside and stayed on solid ground. We were closely online with each other. I could hear both breathing hard. There was a small log lying in our path. We sprang over it, side by side. The short one stumbled and dropped behind.

The tall one and I were side by side as he tried to pull ahead. I was really hurting now, but I grit my teeth, determined that he would not get ahead. I pumped my legs harder. Oh! How I hoped I could see that big old finish log.

I glanced forward. All I saw was somebody waving their arms, jumping up and down and around like a duck with its head chopped off. There were people behind her. The tall one was trying to pull ahead of me. I didn't let him. "Yes!" I heard that wild one yelling and screaming.

I looked up. My heart pumped harder. I spotted those soft, beautiful eyes of no other than Tiekee's. She was all motion and screams. It made my feet fly faster. One more big tree stood in my path, and there was that humongous finish-line log.

A painful thought flashed through my mind: was Tiekee rooting for me or the tall one? I must win either way. I ran harder. The tall one stayed beside me. I must win this race! I pumped even harder. I was just a little bit ahead when the tall one made his leap to clear the log. With all the strength I had left, I lunged with all my might.

As I cleared the log, I saw the tall one's feet hit the log and fly up toward the sky. At the same instant, I clearly heard Tiekee yell, "Thaaangtoook!"

My lead foot hit the ground. I crumpled to the ground totally exhausted, gasping for air. The first person to touch me was Tiekee. Her soft, caressing hands made stars dance in front of me as she brushed my hair from my sweating face. I saw the most beautiful smile ever in my life. I blinked to clear the sweat. She was gone!

There, a finger's length from my nose, was another face. No! It was not Mother. Dakwee had pushed Tiekee away. I struggled to see Tiekee as she sprang to her feet. As she dashed away, she cast a scornful glance at me.

I lost my thoughts. I could not utter a sound! As she streaked quickly away, I believe I spied a small tear in her eye. Dakwee was patting and caressing me as if nothing had happened.

Winning the hatchet could not replace losing Tiekee!

Chapter 11

A World Changed

The festivities, games, visits, and the honoring of the Gods were coming to a close. People were now satisfied that all is well. They were starting to long for their villages and to return to finish preparing for the cold winds ahead. One of the most highly respected young chiefs, Mungset, of the Naniticoke tribe, was exceptionally quiet. He held a troubled look during the entire powwow. He joined the revelers in body, but obviously his mind was elsewhere.

The elder chiefs, sensing that one of their very best young warrior chiefs seemed exceptionally troubled, called a meeting very late the night before the powwow ended. Only the older men attended such meetings. Everyone else was asleep in their brush huts. These meetings were held in a brush arbor with the fire pit centered in the front. The three sides of the arbor were made of small cedar trees, pine boughs, long blades of grass tied into a bundle, and other brush. The open end of the arbor faced to southwest as the prevailing and coldest winds came from the northeast. The steeply slanted roof, supported by poles, was made of similar brush that provided shade and protection from the wind and rain. With the fire burning brightly, the meeting began by the oldest Chief speaking first.

He praised Big God for providing the meat, fruits, vegetables, and the many families to this gathering. He then thanked Big God for the strength, knowledge, and wisdom that He had bestowed upon Mungset. He asked for safety and good health for the rest of the people and closed with a respectful, "Ahkee." All present confirmed agreement with a loud shout of "Ahkee."

He then turned to Mungset, and placing both hands in reassurance on the strong chief's shoulders, looking him directly in the eyes, in a steady voice, he stated, "I have sensed that you, Mungset, one of our strongest and most crafty of the men, are greatly troubled. Please share your troubled burden with us."

Mungset thanked the elder gentleman. Cleared his throat and began. "My fellow braves, you know that I am an honest and reliable warrior. I do not try to make myself to be more or better than any one of you. When I speak, you have come to know that I speak from my heart. I do not have a forked tongue like a snake. I do not add or take away from what I know.

"I ask that you believe me this night as while hunting on the land of the Assateague on the far side of Little Water, I saw a very mysterious family of the strangest animals. I tried to get close to them, but they are as swift as brother and sister deer. In fact, when I first saw them, they were many arrow shots away.

"I moved quietly closer to them as they were eating grass, much as does brother and sister deer. Their heads reminded me of deer. Their bodies are thick, like of brother and sister bear. Their hair is short, except that on the top of their necks. Their tails look like the brush brooms we use to sweep our lodges and the areas around them. Their legs are bigger than brother and sister deer's, but smaller around and longer than brother and sister bear's. Their tracks are round with no toes. They can run as fast as bear and deer. They were afraid of me. They ran away when they saw me. Brothers, never in all the many moons of my time have I seen or heard of such an animal or a spirit."

One of the men asked him to draw on the bare ground a picture of the animals. He took a stick and drew the shape as best he could.

They added grass to the fire to make it cast more light. All studied the shape on the ground in wonder. None had ever seen or heard of such an animal.

Mungset told them that he did not want to alarm the women and children, but these animals are so very strange. He asked, "Did Big God send them or was it the works of some evil spirit?"

The braves agreed that they must keep secret from all in the tribe about what Mungset had seen.

Chief Hicklok very wisely directed, "Do not trouble your squaws and young ones with this. We do not know if these are only a spirit or maybe animal, good nor bad, maybe just different. Several more moons will prove which they are, if they remain to ever be seen again. The strange animals may leave to be seen never again. The Great Spirit may have placed them here among us as a good sign. Their meat may be good as food and their hides good for clothes and blankets. After a few moons we shall know. Say nothing to friend or foe!"

Chapter 12

THE FIRST DEEP SNOW

For the two moons since the big powwow, Tangtok's entire family and their few friends had been busy from daylight to dark gathering edible nuts, roots, and herbs. The braves and older boys had made extra kills of deer and caught plenty of fish. The extra meat was hung over the small fires and smoked for several days while it dried. The squaws and maidens had gathered and dried fruits and vegetables.

A heavy frost had covered the ground almost every morning. Each day the winds grew colder. Mother Earth was forming a hard extra-cold cover. The fresh water would be hard as wood for most of a day or until it was heated over the lodge fire. The saltwater grew hard only at the edges of the shore. The cloaks and blankets of deer hide, the mittens made from rabbit fur, hats made from raccoon and opossum's skin, and the shoes made from muskrat and beaver pelts were a welcomed burden in the freezing cold.

Tangtok woke late this day and lay snuggled in the pile of warm blankets, which had were on a high bed of small pine needles. His thoughts meandered back to when he had last seen the strange animal he had named Bakting because she was so friendly. He did question his mother one time about what animals that were bigger and friendlier than a deer. She told him that only Brothers Bear, Panther and Elk were maybe bigger, but they were not friendly at all. They lived only in Big Forrest on the other side of Little Water, she assured him.

She must have mentioned that to his dad. One day when hunting rabbits and muskrats, his dad, in a joking way, asked him if he had seen any bear or panther on the island. Tangtok made sure he did nothing to arouse his father's suspicions about that strange animal he had seen. All animals and most fish and birds were meat, to be eaten or smoked and then eaten later. Having a secret friend such as Bakting was too good a thing to share. Anyway, who would believe such a story as he would have to tell? Now that the hard work was over, and it was getting cold, maybe it is time to go again and look for his friend.

Several Bright Lights later, he rose and put on the very warmest skins and hides he had. He filled his muskrat hide pouch with some nuts, herbs, the three sisters, and one small piece of smoked fish. With his close friend Mucklit in hand, he moved quickly and quietly into the forest.

Bright Light God was only a dim circle behind hazy clouds. There was a slight breeze from the cold area, but it was not bitter cold. Tangtok planned to move quickly to the south and go beyond where he had earlier found Bakting. Several times since finding her and her friends, he had ventured down to that area, but he had no luck finding her. This time, he would go much farther than ever before.

"Certainly, she was not some spirit and had flown away," he relayed to his stick partner, Mucklit.

Bright Light God was not yet directly overhead when he reached the special copse of trees where he had first met Bakting. Tangtok continued at a brisk pace. He was determined to get to an area that his father and the other men often talked about where clear water gushed from the ground. They claimed that sweet water did not turn into ice and many animals came there to drink. It was known to be visited by a tribe of very mean and fierce people. They killed other people who tried to get water from that spring.

Tangtok knew he had to be very careful while in that area. He did not go out on the beach but stayed in the forest and close to the very thickest parts. Occasionally, he would ease close to the beach to look for tracks. Most of the time, he stayed close to side of Little Water. He constantly searched the large area of marsh grasses that grew between the pocosin forest and Little Water.

Tangtok moved slowly and constantly searched in every direction. He urgently wanted to find his friend. He also was really afraid of being caught by the mean people. Upon reaching a thicket, he stopped and ate some of his food. While standing there, he realized that Bright Light God was now completely hidden by the clouds, which were low and a deep gray. There was a slight breeze, and it was even colder than it had been. He knew that he had little time left before he had to turn back toward home. From the thicket, he could see a nice meadow lying between the forest and the bay. He headed toward it.

Just as he reached the edge of the forest, he came upon a well-traveled path. There in the soft, damp, black dirt, he spied the tracks he had been fervently seeking. Yes! Those are the prints of Bakting's feet. They form a deep, round ring that enclosed a small V. Her feet are smaller than those of her friends. Yes, there are four of them. These had to be made by her!

The young brave stayed off the path while moving rather quickly along. Periodically he would stop and survey the area looking for any enemy and desperately hoping to see the pony. At a soft, marshy spot, the path veered out into the marsh grass, but Bakting's prints did not go out there. She had left the path.

Tracking her now would be much more difficult, but the young man was driven by the excitement that he was close to his long-sought friend. He noticed every spot of grass that had been pressed down. The small bushes the leaves of which had been brushed were noted. He stayed on her trail.

Before realizing it, he was at the edge of wooded area and at the beginning of the sandy beach. He studied the bare area of sand and found no hoofprints. He did see the first fine snowflakes gently flittering down. That was a bad sign! He must soon head for home.

He again searched for Bakting's tracks. He made a little semicircle from the spot he had stopped. Luckily, he found the sign he was seeking. She was heading in the direction he had to go. He followed. The sign led back into the deep woods. He just knew, he could feel, that he was getting close to her. He pushed on into the thick brush. Several times he had to backtrack his steps to find the signs of his friend.

The snow began falling much harder, and it was getting darker. There were places that the tracks were easy to follow. There, he moved quickly. Then he would come upon an area where he could not see any sign.

Oh! How he wished the snow would start sticking so he could easily follow the tracks. Just ahead, he saw a small pond of water. The tracks led into the pond. The water was not very deep, but it was too deep to see any tracks, and the water was clear. That told him that his friend had passed there much earlier than he had been believing. He went around the edge of the pond looking for the place where the cayuse had left the pond. Ice was forming at the edge. He found no tracks.

Now the snow was falling so thick and straight down that he could not tell which direction it was to his lodge. He knew that if he went to the beach, he could find his way home. He had to give up locating his friend and head for the safety of his home. He headed for the beach. He walked in the direction he knew the beach to be. He walked and walked, but no beach. There was no wind or even a breeze. The snow fell straight down. He ate his last food and continued to walk. He came upon what he thought was another pond of water. He circled around the edge of it until he came upon a large tree that had fallen when Big Wind had blown. He remembered crawling over it while trying to find Bakting's tracks. He now knew that he was lost.

He remembered hearing the older braves talking about how White Quiet would come and send one to the White Silent Hole when one was out in such weather. A shelter must be found or made in which to wait out the storm. He again started in the direction he believed to be toward the beach. His clothes had been loosened so he would not sweat. After walking a long time, instead of finding the beach, he came upon a very thick and tangled area of honeysuckle and green briar vines in a thicket of small pine trees. He decided he would make a shelter in these vines among the small pines, wrap up in his furs, and stay until daylight.

It was pitch-black by now as he forced himself slowly into the massive tangles. Luckily, he pushed into the trunk of a large tree that had been blown down. He could not see, but he knew that the best place for him would be close to where the roots were. There he could fashion some sort of a nest at the base of the tree where it joined the upturned roots, which would also be a windbreak.

He started to climb over and through the horizontal limbs of the large tree heading for the upturned roots. He sensed something or heard something that made him stop. Yes! He heard it again. It was a little soft nicker, such as a person very softly chuckling. He waited. Then he caught an odor. It was the same odor as Bakting! He whistled softly.

"Ah-huh-huh-huh," came the soft reply from Bakting.

He knew it was her! She was in the direction he was heading. He crawled slowly under the tangles toward her by feeling along the horizontal trunk of the massive tree. While on his knees, he realized how much his feet were hurting. In fact, he could feel the slippery blood on the bottom of both of his feet. The beaver skin shoes had worn blisters on his toes and heels.

He kept crawling. Finally, he touched the outstretched muzzle of his long sought-after friend. She was under a layer of vines, with dead leaves matted on top of them so thick that no snow fell on her. He removed one mitten and gently rubbed his hand down her neck and gently scratched her shoulder. She was dry and warm. He spoke to her in a soft, gentle tone while thanking both her and the Big God for allowing them to be together in this blizzard.

He slowly crawled under her neck and sat with his back nestled against the log. It was a protected place with no wind and no snow. He could not see the cayuse, but he knew she was standing almost directly over him. The pains in his feet were almost unbearable. He wondered how he would ever make it back to his warm home. He thought about his family and knew they would be upset and worried that he was out in this heavy snowfall. He asked Great God to comfort them and to give him strength. After snuggling in his clothes of hides and furs and pulling the coonskin cap down over his face, he fell into a deep sleep.

Bakting nuzzled Tangtok's head with her warm muzzle. Opening his eyes, he saw in dim dawn light that she was standing directly over him. Ice had formed on the edge of the fur and formed a circle around his mouth and nose. He started to stretch his legs when the pains from his feet shot up both legs. He knew that he could not walk. His feet were not very cold, but the pain from the blisters and sores were almost unbearable. The breath from both him and Bakting caused a slight fog to form in their natural shelter.

Looking out from under Bakting's belly, he could see that it was still snowing. He could tell that the snow was already as high as his hips. He thought of his family and their warm fire. He felt in the pouch and found a few beans. Grabbing a fistful, he took some in one hand and offered the rest to his protecting friend with an outstretched hand, palm up. Bakting softly nibbled the morsels. Her big soft eyes and her ears gently rolled forward, all focusing directly on him, as though wondering why he was here.

The protection provided by the overhanging mat of vines and leaves, the trunk, and the upturned roots made a cozy little hutch. The warmth from their two bodies warded off some of the chill. The wind was still moving the few branches that could be seen. The snow was falling so thick that only the trunks of the nearest trees could be seen. The falling snow blanked out everything past one short stone throw.

Tangtok begin to realize that he was in very serious trouble. He was not able to walk even if there was no snow. He thought even if his family and others of their tribe could move in this deep snow, they had no idea of where to begin to look. Oh, why had he not told someone where he was going? As long as he didn't move his feet or wiggle his toes, the pain was not terribly bad. He thanked the Big God that, at least, he was not freezing.

Only one more good handful of beans and corn were left. He felt the last piece of smoked fish. He mumbled some things to Bakting and thanked her again for being here with him. Being warm and in serene silence, sleep overtook him again.

Bakting's movement awoke him. He cleared away a small hole and looked out. It had stopped snowing. He guessed that Bright Light God was probably about directly overhead. The low clouds were steel gray and were moving very slowly. Tangtok remembered that such clouds may very well turn to snow again when it became dark. Then the bitter, deep cold would sit in. He had to make it to the protection of his home and the warm fire.

He started to stand up. The pains from his feet made his knees so weak that he slumped back down. He struggled to get back up. He had to walk.

The Silent Hole took animals and birds that failed to find shelter. The Silent Hole would take him too if he stayed out here until the bitter cold came whistling in on the wind. That was certain to happen very soon. He finally forced himself to stand. Bakting perked up her ears and shook her head as if to say, "Let's go! You can do it."

The young warrior took a step. He went down to his knees. Again, he struggled up and leaned on the side of Bakting. She very slowly took a step toward the opening. He held on to her mane and made a small step. She moved again. He made another step. The pain did not subside. The horse moved slowly again. He took another step. The pain made the young brave wonder if he would live to see dark.

Bakting stepped into the snow. It was up to her stomach. Tangtok realized that he could not walk in that deep blanket of solid snow.

Bakting slowly swung her head around and fixed a questioning look at him, standing there with a look of horrid despair on his face. She shifted her look to over her back. Tangtok followed her line of sight. He hung his body over her back to get the pain from his feet to let up. As his weight settled on her back, Bakting moved gently forward into the snow. The boy's feet dragged along beside her. She kept moving. He kept clinging on, knowing that if he fell off that he would surely be overcome by the cold.

Bakting continued at a slow, steady pace. They came to a small rivulet of moving, fresh water. Ice was beginning to form along the edges. The mare stopped, slightly bent one knee so her mouth could reach the water, and sucked up several long draughts of the crystal-clear water. As she lifted her head, the water on the whiskers of her muzzle froze into little balls. It was getting colder.

She then turned and followed her tracks back to the shelter the way they had come. The young warrior could do nothing more than remain slumped, motionless over her warm body

Tangtok wished he had stayed in the shelter. His second thoughts were that the cozy spot would be where he would slip into the Silent Hole. The snow stopped falling, and the wind begin to blow. The trees and the brush kept the snow from drifting around them.

Just as they came into sight of the shelter where they had spent the last eighteen hours, the pony veered off to go around the fallen tree. Tangtok was getting tired from clinging onto the horse while dangling head down over her back. As his feet slipped down a little, the mare stopped and slowly turned to gaze at her weakened friend. Tangtok realized that his only hope was to get up and sit, straddle-legged, on his strong friend's back.

Would she allow him to do that? He firmly grasped a fistful of her long mane and forced himself to swing one leg over her back. She stood steady as a rock. He squirmed a little to settle down on her and grasped her mane with both hands as he hunched over her neck. She then lowered her head and started off in a determined walk.

The boy did not know where she was headed. But wherever it was, he knew that he had to stay with her, or he would perish in the cold. Soon, he realized that she was coming to the beach of Big Water. She stepped out of the forest onto the slightly frozen sand. The wind had swept the beach clear of most of the snow. She stopped and looked both left and right, as to say which way now.

Tangtok knew that if he kept Big Water on his side in the direction that Bright Light God climbed up from under, and keep the forest on the side that Bright Light God crawled back under, he would get to his home and his family. The boy tugged at her mane and pointed her toward his home. The mare started in a brisk walk. After a few minutes, she began to trot. The shaking caused the boy's feet to hurt a little more, but he knew he was getting closer to home. Although he did not recognize any of the area, he knew he was heading in the right direction. He let out a little yell of joy.

Bakting took that to mean he wanted to go faster. She broke into a rocking gallop. The frigid winter wind made tears run from both of Tangtok's eyes. While his feet were throbbing in pain, his heart was thumping in joy. The horse thundered on swiftly over the frozen ground.

Yes! Yes! Tantok finally saw some trees and parts of the beach that he recognized. Bakting kept up the pace. Then smoke from the home came into sight. No tracks were in the snow. His family had not ventured out into such a terrible storm. When there was only one tree between the pair and the boy's house, the horse stopped. Tangtok needed to get closer to the house as his feet were still too painful to walk on. He urged the horse forward. She took a timid step, and then suddenly, she whirled and leaped in the direction they had just come.

The boy fell into some brush that was covered in snow. As he looked up, he saw his friend was dashing down the beach in a sweeping gallop and was out of sight by the time he forced himself to stand. He was alone in the blowing cold wind and the hip-deep snow, but was within a stone's throw of his house. He yelled at the top of his voice. The wind drowned out his voice. He yelled again. No answer.

He started crawling. The snow was so deep that he could not move forward. He tried again to stand and force his way the through snow. He made it a few feet when the pain and lack of breath made him slump down. He yelled again. Again, no answer. The wind was howling and getting colder by the minute. It was getting dark.

A deep chill shuddered through him. Now the pains in his feet were ebbing away. In fact, he was feeling a little warmer, he thought. Little did he know, but this is the early signs of one going into White Quiet. Silent Hole. It would then swallow him as darkness covered the Mother Earth.

As he lay facedown on the snow, his hand felt one of the small rocks that formed a circle around the outside fire pit. He clutched the rock in his throwing hand, and pushed himself up onto his knees. With all his might, he threw the small rock as hard as he could. The days he had spent for the past several years throwing rocks and sticks at everything he could think of, from clumps of grass to rabbits and even birds, served him well.

The rock hit the stiff hide that covered the doorway. Immediately his mother's face poked out. He yelled again. Her face slipped back into the house. She must not have heard him! He fell in total despair.

Why is his father slapping his face and yelling at him? This is only a silly dream. The boy murmured to himself, "Go back to sleep." Then he felt Big God, he thought, pick him up to take him to the Silent Hole. When his body hit his father's strong shoulder and he smelled the familiar odor of his dad, he knew that this was not Big God.

The next thing he knew, he was on a pile of warm furs, next to the fire in the center of his home. Everyone was shouting and laughing and patting him in glee. It was a great reunion!

Everyone was asking questions at the same time. Tangtok was in a real dilemma. Could he dare attempt to tell what had actually happened? Who would believe such a tale? Also, if he revealed that Bakting was in the area, would his father or some of the other men hunt her down for meat to eat? He was raised in a culture that demanded that one must always be truthful. Lives depended on the truth being known. His tribe depended on knowing the truth about events. Lying, being deceptive, or misleading others usually caused bad decisions and all suffering from it.

"What must I say?" he asked himself. Truth is the only way! "Must one always tell the truth, even if it will cause his best friend to die?"

The young man took full the advantage of all the commotion and excitement and the fact that he did feel very weak and tired. Once in a while, he moaned a little and said nothing.

Chapter 13

LIVING A LIE

After Backting saved Tangtok during the Deep Snow, Tangtok could not force himself to tell what had happened, and he could not force himself to stop thinking about and admiring what the pony had done for him. He often left his hut area for the entire day. He would hunt squirrels, rabbits, other small game and he would gather oysters from the shore, but his parents were not happy with how little he brought home. They were happy that he had lived through the Deep Snow, confused about how he did that, and very concerned that he was a much different boy after that near tragedy.

Tangtok was consumed by the desire to see and visit with the four-legged friend who had saved his life, and was much troubled by the fact that he could not bring himself to tell others what had happened.

Three Pale-Face Lights after the Big Snow, he finally had the willpower to share with his older sister, Loru, what had taken place. Before confessing to her, he asked her to make a blood promise to keep a secret. She agreed. They both cut their little finger of the right hand with a clamshell, touched their bloody fingers together to seal the secret between them. Now, that secret must remain between only them, even if all their blood and their life is drained from their body in protecting that secret.

Loru loved her little brother. She made him comfortable about what he told and why it seemed so hard to share to adults what had happened. She encouraged him to keep visiting his life-saving friend. He did, even though he was scolded often by his parents for being lazy.

During one of his extra-long hunts, he spied the animal which meant so much to him. It took a little time to get close to her as she was grazing out in the marsh. Finally, she saw him working his way around the patches of tall cattails, which grew only in the softest mud. At first, she held her head high, pointed both ears directly toward him, and flared her nostrils to get more air if she needed to run and to help catch an odor of what was approaching. He stopped and softly whistled.

The stiffness in her quickly relaxed. She let out a short, soft whinny, tossed her head, and waved her long mane up and down in a friendly manner. She started moving slowly toward him. They met, cautiously, on a small hammock of marsh grass. Tangtok offered her some corn and beans. The pony eased up to him and nibbled the morsels from his upheld, open palm. He spoke in a very soft, smooth voice to her as she ate.

When she finished, he stepped closer to her and began scratching her neck and withers. That felt so good to her as it removed some of the long, dead hair that had been her cold season coat. He continued to scratch and rub her back. It was a most pleasant time for both.

Finally, he had to start back toward home. The mare followed along behind. He was surprised and so happy that he could hardly remain calm—his friend was following him! He did not want to frighten away his most dear friend. Every once in a while, he would stop, speak softly to her, and scratch or rub her. Even after all the corn and beans were gone, she would nuzzle his pouch, looking for more of the goodies. She followed him until he could smell the smoke of his lodge. It was almost dark.

She stopped, turned around, took a few steps, curved her neck around so she could look directly at him, and shook her head sideways as if to say, "I don't like this." He spoke firmly but softly to her, saying,

"Everything will be all right now that we have found each other." He moved out toward his home, skipping along, so happy that he had again found his very best friend in this whole world.

From then on, they met each other every few Bright Lights. After a few meetings, he again got on her back. She would walk along with him sitting on her back talking to her and sometimes singing some of his favorite songs. They became bonded only as true friends can.

Chapter 14

A Life Sealed, Forever!

The hot season passed slowly. Tangtok spent hours at a time riding Bakting. They totally enjoyed their time together. Most of the time, the rides were slow walking, easy trips. Sometimes they became wild dashes through the woods or on the beach. When they frightened a rabbit or a fox, Tangtok urged Bakting to give chase. The rides became wild, hectic races.

As time passed, they learned a language between them. Bakting learned when Tangtok pushed a hand against her neck, she was to turn away from the pressure. When he tapped her ribs with his heels, she was to pick up speed; the more he tapped, the faster she ran. Of course, she also knew when chasing an animal how to stay right behind the animal with no directions from Tangtok. She learned several of his voice commands. Making a clicking noise meant to move. Commanding, "Hoak, hoak," and tugging back on her mane meant to slow down or to stop.

When Tangtok threw Mucklit and missed, she knew to go to the stick and stop. Sometimes she stopped so quickly that Tangtok took a nosedive over her head. He always broke into a loud laugh when that happened. She would cast a whimsical look at him of, "Duh! You are the one who missed!" Also, when Mucklit struck a target, she knew to get beside the wounded animal quickly so Tangtok could finish it off with the small club he carried tucked into his loincloth. When he shot an arrow, she stood still, or when running, she ran as smooth and straight as possible. They became a well-trained team.

Chasing the small animals became much more than just fun. Tangtok quickly learned that using Mucklit as a weapon brought needed meat and hides for the family. The entire village soon learned that Tangtok was becoming a highly respected hunter. Every two or three Bright Lights, he would return home with several animals in his sack that were so necessary for his family's well-being. Realizing that he was becoming well respected only increased Tangtok's concern for the safety of his dearest friend, Bakting. It was time to confess to the entire village how he had become the greatest provider.

How to do this and keep Bakting safe was a serious challenge. He first asked Sister Loru to come with him to tell his father. After a polite discussion between the three of them, it was agreed that Bakting was the main reason Tangtok was so successful. She and her kind were certainly a special and great gift from Big God. Father also knew of no animal, large or small, that his people saw as anything other than a gift to eat and to use their hides for warmth and protection. That was the way of his people. He decided that he must first witness Tangtok and Bakting working as one, before he would go the chiefs about this new discovery. Until then, all this must remain a tight secret between the three of them. Not even Mother can learn of their plan.

Several Bright Lights later, Father told Tangtok that Rain God will come and hide Bright Light God. That will be a good time to hunt together. Tangtok agreed. Unfortunately, sleep would not come for Tangtok. He had many visions as he lay on his sleeping mound. Would Bakling allow him to get close with Father being there? Would they find game? Everything must go perfectly for Father to be convinced that Bakting must be allowed to live.

The rain began sprinkling as Father and Tangtok left their cozy home. The hot season was giving way to cool times, but the rain was not cold. They moved swiftly down the beach. Two arrow shots distance of walking, and those chubby red ears poked out from some tall Myrtle bushes. Father froze in his tracks. Bakting slowly emerged from the bushes and turned her head toward the two-legs-no-feathers as if to say, "I have been waiting for you slowpokes."

Father gasped at what he saw. The animal was beautifully marked, with white patches and dark blotches of shining hair. The long hair on her neck was partially white and black. Her broom-shaped tail was mostly black, as was the hair around the bottom of her stout, muscular legs. She was obviously alert yet calm. Her back was as high as his chest. She was taller than a bear and had only posts for feet, with no toes. Yes! This is cayuse, as the wise medicine man had described and as Chief Mungset had told about.

"What a magnificent animal," Father said to himself. "This animal has too kind of a spirit to become meat to eat. No one who ever saw her would be comfortable wearing her skin."

Father slowly stepped towards her. She met his eyes with those big soft, gentle eyes of hers. His heart melted. Bakting was a divine friend of his from that day until the Dark Hole took him. Many, old and young, relished him describing this experience many times around many campfires. This tough, hard hunter was so humbled by this kind creature.

Tangtok quickly realized that great respect passed between his father and Bakting. What a great relief it was to him for this to happen when it happened. Now he, Bakting, and Mucklit had one more tough test to pass: they must show how they caught game.

After greeting Bakting with their usual scratching and rubbing, while she pranced around nipping at him and Mucklit, Tangtok smoothly swung a leg up and over Bakting's back, as he had done many times. He caught sight of Father standing there, as if frozen. Pushing his hand against Bakting's neck and clucking to her, she spun gently around to face Father.

His eyes almost popped from their sockets. That was too much, too quick for the seasoned hunter to believe, even though he knew this was not a dream. Tangtok, overjoyed with all that had just happened, as casual as he could do it, mentioned it was time for the hunters to go catch game.

The rain fell a little harder. That was not the very best for hunting, as the animals would be snuggled in nests and hiding spots. After checking—with no luck—several bushy areas where rabbits usually sit, the rain stopped. Bright Light God showed his round, warm face. Varmints of every kind started scurrying around.

A long story made short: After Tangtok's boasting and bragging about always catching more than they could carry, it dawned on him that Father did not seem impressed. There was nothing in the sack.

"Don't let a big bear's bite grab more than a little rabbit's mouth can chew" flashed through Tangtok's mind. Why does my tongue wag while my brain sleeps? Oh, why?

As usual, Big God did bless their hunt with several rabbits, a muskrat, and two big, fat raccoons. Father was truly impressed and overjoyed that his boy, who now was obviously a strong, able young man, had accomplished so much with his close friend Bakting.

The village meeting area was packed with people, both the old and the young, and a big fire was blazing. Many who seldom came to tribal meetings were there. Everyone who had a special part in the village's life, and their families, were at this meeting. The word was out that a great new discovery was to be revealed.

The highest chief opened the meeting with the usual prayers, thanksgivings, and social recognitions. He directed that no comments or questions were to be made until the next speaker finished his presentation. With that said, he invited Tangtok's father to speak.

Father's enthusiasm and sincerity brought a quiet silence over the entire crowd. He explained all that had gone through Tangtok's life for the past two hot seasons, and how Bakting had enabled him to catch more than ample provisions. He described how powerful and fast Bakting was. His description of her spirit convinced the crowd that Bakting was a sister-spirit to people and that no one would ever be comfortable wearing her hide or eating her meat.

Father closed by asking that all who agreed that Bakting and her kind were to be treated as kin to people, to stand and state "Aikee." The sound of their voices rolled like thunder across the waters on both sides of the long island.

Chapter 15

WHERE THERE IS A WILL, THERE IS A WAY!

For several hot seasons, the big powwows were cancelled because there was a war taking place. Small hunting parties of the Cold Nation people were coming as close as two Bright Light walks from the sweet, flowing water of the Pocomoke. Cold Nation country was one Pale-Face Light walk away from the Pocomoke River. The Cold Nation people believed they had the power to hunt and raid when and where they chose. So they used the power they had.

The Choptank, Naniticoke, and Assateague were quiet, peaceful people who believed in "Live and let live." A hunting raid usually resulted in only threats. A raid capturing squaws, maidens, and children was one step too far. It meant counterraids would follow. Hunting raids by Cold Nation continued through the cold season, when water became harder than wood.

Early in the beginning of the warm season, the key chiefs of the local tribes who participated in the Big Powwow along the Pocomoke River called a War Council. Cold Nation had gone too far by capturing a young squaw and two of her maidens. Several scouting parties by the Choptanks had travelled secretly deep into Cold Nation country to learn where the captured squaw and her young were being held. They learned nothing. Thus, the local chiefs now decided that war must be declared and fought to win.

The call went out for the most capable hunters to meet at the Pocomoke Powwow area to train as warriors. Squaws with no children and unmarried maidens were asked to volunteer to join the war effort by maintaining the training area, gathering and preparing food, and learning to treat the injured or wounded. Thus, the elderly, mothers with young children, and the infirm were left to maintain the home villages.

The War Chief of Tangtok's village spoke to Tangtok and his father about a big advantage it would be for Tangtok and Bakting to join the war effort as a team, based on their successes as hunters. Because there was no canoe that could carry Bakting or that she would ride in, Tangtok and Bakting walked to the Chincoteague village where Bakting could swim the narrow channel and get on the mainland. Thus, by the time Tangtok and Bakting made it to the pow-wow grounds, five Bright Lights after most had arrived, every person there had learned of, and was extremely anxious to see, this amazing animal that was a close friend of people.

The five days of walking allowed much thinking about who would be at the grounds. What would his friends look like? Tangtok knew he had grown and was much more muscular than he was during the earlier powwows, now three or four hot seasons latter. Dakwee had left her village before he arrived and was probably already at the grounds. Would Tiekee be there? Knowing how maidens can be, they both have most likely found another boy to be their best friend. To his surprise, Dakwee was the very first to see him arrive.

At her alert, many of his friends came running behind her. She froze in her tracks, as did the rest of the crowd, when Bakting stepped from behind Tangtok. The animal was much bigger than they had envisioned. Everyone was interested in the animal. After some cautiously approached and finally greeted Tangtok, all wanted to touch Bakting.

It was a merry gathering of excited people. The crowd of young people followed Tangtok and Bakting into the middle of the village. All the chiefs met Tangtok and rendered the sign of deep respect to him by tapping first their fist to their chest and then soundly tapping Tangtok's chest. Dakwee stood beside Tangtok, her face beaming with pride. When all the chiefs had honored Tangtok, the older braves, followed by the younger ones, did likewise. Bakting and Tangtok were welcomed in a most regal manner. But where were Tiekee and her brother?

The chiefs wasted no time to begin training. Several parties were formed under various chiefs. Every brave, squaw, and maiden had to train in personal defense: how to fight hand-to-hand, how to use a tomahawk with skill, and how to shoot arrows quickly and accurately. War parties consist of three groups: One group is the hunter-gatherers, which includes the squaws, maidens, and a few of the less able men. They provide and prepare the food and offer medical care.

The scouts form one group. They operate secretly in two or three-man teams and were the experts in navigation, living off the land, and sneaking in and around groups of the enemy.

Warriors form the largest group. They are the strongest who never quit and are good at and relish fighting.

The chiefs divide them into teams. They become like brothers to each other. Of course, every group would join in the battle when necessary. Each group and team had a chief. The two highest chiefs were the Warrior Chief and the Medicine Chief. The Warrior Chief was the highest leader of all others. Medicine Chief was a close advisor to all chiefs. He was wise about the ways of people and of the spirits.

Much time was spent in training Bakting. She seemed to really enjoy the attention and care. Everyone had a little snack of corn or beans for her. She was trained to lie down and be still. She learned "Stay" and to "Come" only when Tangtok and one of two chiefs whistled or gave the command, no matter who or why any other whistled or commanded. When given the command to "go home," she would immediately trot to the campsite, but only when Tangtok and one of the same two chiefs gave that command. While Tangtok was on her back, it came naturally for her to charge a brave, no matter how he dodged or ran, and stay after him until he was caught. The pair became a formidable fighting team. The other braves worked hard to earn the right to fight alongside the inseparable pair.

During the first few Bright Lights of training, Tangtok tried hard to learn why Tiekee and her brother were missing. Dakwee let it be known quickly that she did not want to hear anything about those two, and especially so about Tiekee. Eventually, Tangtok learned that a party from Tiekee's village was on a long trip visiting other tribes asking them to join the war against the Cold Nation. As the son and the daughter of the High Choptank Chief, they were representing their father, who was at the Pocomoke training grounds. He was a strict, professional warrior. He not only visited most of the training but also often demonstrated the actions that he required to be followed. He was a very powerful brave who could run and fight mock battles longer than any other. He taught different methods of getting close to the enemy and surprising them. He believed in attacking from two directions, in circling around the enemy and making the enemy fight in two directions. He and the Medicine Chief came up with various maneuvers in attacking. His wisdom was sound. All held him in high respect.

Chapter 16

WAR IS NO GAME

After several weeks of hard training, the order was given to break camp and move toward the Cold Nation country. Scouts to the front. One team of warriors was to always be the rear guard. Each chief to be the lead person in his team. The Highest Chief would be close behind the scouts and in the front of the lead warrior team. The Medicine Chief went where he believed he was needed. No one knew when or where they would meet the enemy. Everyone knew that they would move until they met the enemy and drew blood. This is a life-or-death situation. When a tribe has power and does not use it, that tribe has no power. If all people had enough strength to resist greed, there would be no war.

Many Bright Lights later, all in the party knew they were in Cold Nation country as the hills were very high. The rivers between them were shallow and flowed very fast in many places, allowing easy crossing. The routine had been this: move several Bright Lights at a brisk pace, rest only when dark, then camp on a hill for several days while several teams went scouting for the enemy and foraging for food. So far, all the people contacted were friendly and feared the Cold Nation people.

Soon after Bright Light God showed his face at the last camp, a party of friendly hunters very cautiously approached the camp. They met with several of the chiefs and shared some very sad news. They appeared to be very frightened and on edge. They related in a halting manner that about half of their women and children had been captured and carried away by the Cold Nation people. Their party was the last of the young men left alive. Their village set at the very beginning of the big water known as Chesapeake. Every hut in their entire village had been burned.

They shared that the Cold Nation chiefs told their old men and squaws to move to warm country or they too shall be sent to the Silent Hole. A frightened look shot across their faces when Bakting walked into sight. They looked around bewildered and clamped shut their mouths as they indicated they had to leave. After much pleading with them and offering them hot stew to eat, they slightly relaxed.

No one spoke until they finished eating. Their eyes never left Bakting. The Medicine Chief walked over to Bakting and greeted her with the usual scratching and petting. The oldest of the visitors watched every move that the Medicine Chief made. One visitor spoke in a very timid, soft voice as he said, "Great Medicine Chief, you have great power and wisdom. Did you know or are you the same Medicine man who was with us for longer than one Pale-Face light? He had been captured by Cold Nation before burning our village."

Medicine Chief responded, "I know him not. I am only me. I am not him."

The friendly brave continued, "He told us that he had come many Pale-Face lights of walking from across the mountains and the mighty river far, far from here. He walked in the direction that Bright Light God rose up from. He claimed that in the direction of where Bright Light slips under, several Pale-Face Lights of walking from here, was big-sky country because it was many, many arrow shots across. There, the Comanche and Cheyenne people keep animals as that one." He pointed to Bakting. "During his talk, we had been confused and did not know to believe or not believe. Now we believe. Big God is powerful and good."

After an uncomfortable silence, Medicine Chief rose and placed his hands on the shoulders of the visitor who had spoken and said, "You have suffered much. You have seen much that is not understood. Our spirit calls to you. Be strong, be brave, Depart in peace."

The visitors stood to leave. As they stepped off to go, the one who spoke took a deep breath and, showing much fear, blurted out, "Chief, do us no harm! We came to ask that you come to where we slept. There lies a warrior we believe to be of your people. We do not know him. We did not harm him. The Cold Nation believed they had sent him to the Silent Hole. He did not go. We did not do this. He needs medicine and help. Will you come?"

Medicine Chief, realizing now why they had shown so much fear for their lives, quickly agreed. The Chief calmed their fears by assuring them he believed they had not harmed the wounded one. He summoned several braves, Tangtok, and Bakting and directed that they follow the visitor and bring back the wounded warrior.

The Medicine Chief sent them off with a warning. "I trust this visitor, but believe nothing you hear from him and only half of what you see. Be wise, be cautious. Do not be tricked!"

The team travelled about four long arrow shots when they were led into a scattered camp of several disheveled old braves and old squaws. Next to the stream on a mossy knoll, under a large deerskin blanket, lay the wounded warrior. Tangtok lifted the blanket from the lifeless form. He dropped the blanket in surprise and anguish. It was no other than Tiekee's brother, Mookwig, the High Chief's son, whom Tangtok had defeated in the wrestling match several years earlier.

Mookwig was covered with cuts, lumps, bruises, and clots of blood. His head had been severely beaten. His swollen eyes were only slightly opened. His breathing was an irregular, weak gasp of air. He only moaned a little when Tangtok lifted one of his hands and asked him to wake up.

The young brave was in very poor shape, maybe slipping into the Silent Hole.

A litter of two extra-long poles and the deer skin was made. The extended poles were lashed together by a vine long enough for the poles to hang snugly along each side of Bakting's body. They gently placed the wounded brave on the litter, lifted the litter up, and lowered the long poles onto Bakting until the vines held the poles just below her backbone. Two braves placed the other end of a pole on one of their shoulders. The party left in a trot.

One in the party quickly ran ahead and alerted the squaws to get water heated and for some to go gather medicine plants used to heal wounds. Dakwee prepared a soft bed and gathered a couple of bobcat hide blankets to cover the wounded. Dakwee became Mookwig's primary caregiver. His father made certain that he was treated with healing medicine and slowly fed broth and stew through a River Reed tube. Dakwee would suck the broth or stew up into the reed tube, place her finger over the end of the tube, then allow the liquid to very slowly seep into Mookwig's mouth. It was slow, tedious work. Each day he grew stronger. Several Bright Lights later, Mookwig slowly gained consciousness.

Then the worst news came out: Tiekee had been captured and carried away, to where no one knew.

As Mookwig regained his health and strength, his friendship also grew with Tangtok and especially so with Dakwee. He and Tangtok became warrior brothers. His father tolerated that, but his closeness with Dakwee did not sit well with the stern old Chief. Tangtok and Dakwee were made to clearly understand that no Choptank, brave or maiden, would ever be allowed to marry an Assateague. That just would not happen.

Several clashes with the Cold Nation parties occurred. The Cold Nation warriors were no match for the peace-loving braves under their warrior leaders. In every instance, the Cold Nation suffered many losses. Several braves earned high recognition for their actions against the enemy, especially Tangtok and Bakting. Their feats were often discussed with pride and light-heartedness at night around the campfire. Those stories would be recounted often around other campfires for years to come.

Chapter 17

BIG GOD PROVIDES A WAY

The raiding and warfare continued until it was mid-hot season without learning where Tiekee was being held. Dakwee had obviously gained very strong feelings for Mookwig, who was demonstrating his abilities to become a great chief, such as his father. He, Dakwee, Tangtok, and Bakting had become a close-knit team. When you saw one, you saw the others close by, even on raids.

Tangtok was happy for both Mookwig and Dakwee becoming very close friends. He had Bakting, and his heart longed for Tiekee. Often, the conversation between the three two-legs-no-feathers centered around the revelation about other tribes far, far away, having cayuses. The next most-often subject between them was how Mookwig's father was against the Assateagues. In any case, they were determined to find and retrieve Tiekee.

Many plans and ideas passed between the three about what may happen when they get Tiekee back. For certain, the raids and the war will stop, as much blood had been shed, mostly by the Cold Nation. The hunting raids were still exciting.

The war raids were becoming old. The Cold Nation had learned they were no match for the peace-loving people of the warm country. When a Cold Country band was found, the band quickly split up and ran to escape and evade as individuals. Many were captured and extremely tortured because they did not know the whereabouts of Tiekee. This was dampening the morale and enthusiasm of the attackers. Some were losing their spirit to fight.

During a hunting raid, Dakwee discovered movement inside Bakting. That could mean only one thing: Bakting was going to have a baby. That also confirmed the real possibility of the other cayuses on the home island also may be carrying or may have a foal. This led to many happy conversations about what that could lead to. Mookwig was becoming very certain that he was going back to Assateague to learn more about Bakting's kind, or at least that was what he claimed. He often mentioned that his people must become friends with cayuses and work with them as they had been working so successfully with Bakting. Cayuses must never become animals to hunt and kill.

While on a hunt, the scouts contacted them and alerted that they had found a large village of North Country people on the far said of the Susquehanna River. The village was two Bright Lights travel toward where Bright Light God slipped below the trees. The scouts were convinced that if that large enemy village learned of the warm country party, they would attack and kill everyone. The hunting party and the scouts quickly returned to their main camp.

A very long meeting followed. The scouts' advice pre-vailed. They must strike camp and begin returning to the warm country. Mookwig and Tangtok were angry with the decision. Mookwig met with his father. He respectfully told his dad that he was not going to return until he made one last attempt to find his sister. If he found her, he was going to then return to Dakwee's home to be with her and to learn more about Bakting's kind.

His father said, "I believe you will go to the Silent Hole before you find my daughter. Maybe she is safe and happy where she now stands. From where Pale-Face Light God now stands, I shall forbid again no more forever7 your right to choose your own way. Be strong. Be brave."

Mookwig met with Tangtok and Dakwee, and told them his father allowed him to continue to look for Tiekee.

Dakwee firmly stated, "Our fate is sealed together. Where you lead, I follow until the Silent Hole takes one or both of us."

Tangtok confirmed that he could not and would not return to the Assateague without talking to Tiekee. He said, "She may be the happy squaw of another. Until she tells me so, I can do no less than find her, wherever she stands."

As Bright Light God began to peek through the trees, Mookwig, Dakwee, Tangtok, and Bakting stood and solemnly watched as the War Party began the long trek to the warm country. Once the last warrior was out of sight, the four turned their backs toward Bright Light God and headed toward the big river. They moved cautiously as they were alone in enemy territory.

Upon reaching the river, they learned that it was wide and deep. They quietly moved in the woods up the river listening for rushing rapids. That will be shallow water that can be waded through. They would cross only during dark. The next Bright Light found them on the far side of the river. There was much sign of people on a trail. From the sign of the top footprints, they learned the village was upstream. They found a ravine with a thicket in it. They spread apart so each one would make as little of a trail as possible. They waited in the shade until dark.

After slowly moving two long arrow shots, they smelled campfire smoke. They moved closer until they clearly heard voices. Mookwig whispered to move into the brush. He told them to wait as he would take a closer look. After a long wait, he returned and had them move farther from the trail. He had picked out two braves who appeared to be chiefs. He saw several squaws and maidens, but no sign of Tiekee. Dark had recently fallen, so there was still a lot of activity in the village. Tangtok asked that they move away from the river and try to find a high spot above the village where they could observe it during Bright Light.

Mookwig took the lead. Dakwee was behind him. Bakting followed her, with Tangtok being the rear guard. As they moved up and away from the river, the woods thinned out into a grove of large oak trees. That made moving easier and less noisy. They followed a ridge up to where it joined another one. When Bright Light God started coming into sight, they could tell there was no sign of people travelling in this area.

They found some berries in the ravine, and Tangtok shot a rabbit and two squirrels with arrows. They gathered squaw wood (dead limbs still on the tree that make very little smoke), dug a small hole with sticks, started the fire, and cooked the game. The fire was in the hole so only a little of it could be detected. Only a very fine wisp of smoke appeared. Later, they found just above them a hidden open meadow that had been, a long time ago, a beaver pond.

They discussed several plans of how to best learn who was or was not in that village. The lowest hut was just a short distance from the river. Most of the huts were strung out along the hillside on a flat area well above the river. A wide trail ran through the center of the village. They knew they did not want to get caught between the village and the river.

They kept searching the village for any sign of Tiekee, realizing that she may not be in this village. Most of the braves left the village to hunt and fish. Some went upriver, and some went down. Many had fish traps made of sticks and vines. There were squaws, maidens, and young braves moving about in the village, but no sign of Tiekee.

Tangtok devised a plan to capture one of the chiefs. Once captured, he could be forced to reveal what he knew about Tiekee. The plan was that he and Bakting would move after dark as close to the village as possible without being discovered. At an opportune time, with Tangtok mounted, they would charge into the village at full speed. Tangtok would club one of the chiefs, knock him unconscious, throw the chief over Bakting's back, with the chief's body in front of Tangtok, and tightly grasp Bakting's mane and dash out of the village going downhill. Mookwig would be on the trail waiting. When Bakting approaches, Mookwig will step out and grab Bakting's mane close to her ears, turn her away from the river, and help her climb up the hill. The three of them would go as fast as possible to the upper end of the meadow, which they had recently found. To make certain the plan would work, they did a rehearsal in the meadow.

Mookwig was the unconscious chief during the rehearsal. Dakwee acted the part of Mookwig. They did a walk-through. It went well. Then they did one at half-speed. They decided to make an improvement— Dakwee would be at the trail and grab Bakting's mane to guide her and help her up to the meadow. Mookwig would get behind Bakting as a rear guard. Tangtok learned exactly how he had to lean on the body draped over Bakting to keep it from sliding off. If Tiekee was discovered, they would follow the same plan, only Tangtok would place Tiekee on Bakting, sitting up with her legs straddling Bakting.

They ate the rest of the meat while Bakting grazed in the hidden meadow and then all rested until Bright Light God slide under the trees.

As dark came, they moved slowly toward the upper end of the village. When they came close to the trail, they heard voices coming from the village. They paused and listened to the sounds. Mookwig and Dakwee left to circle around the village on the uphill side. When in place, Mookwig would mock the call of an owl. Tangtok commanded Bakting to "stay." He moved to a spot where he could observe down the trail through most of the village. Several campfires were providing good light. He spied several maids. His heart skipped a beat as he caught his breath. He let the air escape a little too loud. There was no Tiekee in sight.

An owl hooted up on the side of the hill. Big God was helping them, as Mookwig would not utter a sound until he was at the far end of the village. Tangtok saw several braves gather around the middle fire. An older, very muscular brave joined them. Those at the fire gave him the sign of honor by tapping chests. Why couldn't he have been an older and smaller chief? In a short time, another brave joined the crowd. He was obviously much older. All stepped aside and allowed him to get close to the fire. Tangtok decided the one on the outside of the group was the one easiest to get to. He waited for the owl to hoot from Mookwig.

The strong chief turned as if he were leaving. Tangtok mounted Bakting and eased her onto the trail. It was now or never! He vigorously tapped Bakting's flanks. She kicked up stones, lunging out in a full gallop. As they passed the first fire, the owl hooted, straight ahead. Squaws and children screamed as they dashed for cover. Those around the middle fire acted as though nothing was amiss until one looked up and saw this odd animal with what appeared to be a man on its back coming fast as a bird toward them. He froze motionless.

The muscular chief heard thunder coming toward him and turned to look. Too late! The club hit him just above his ear. He reeled over toward Bakting as she slid to a halt. It was perfect timing. Tangtok grabbed the slumping chief and, with a heave, threw him over Bakting's back. The chief's body was in front of Tangtok, who reached over the chief's back, grabbed a fistful of mane, and clucked loudly for Bakting to take off in a full gallop.

Tangtok's feet were hitting ground in extra-long strides, way far apart, as he could not run as fast as Bakting was galloping.

Everyone else just stood frozen in place. Not one could move. They had never seen or heard of such an animal. It was half-man and half—some strange creature.

Dakwee whistled just before stepping onto the trail. Bakting slowed her pace as Dakwee's hand grabbed the hair of her mane just behind the ear and gently guided Bakting away from the river and up the hill. As the brush closed behind them, Mookwig stepped onto the trail. He paused for a second, Yes. He heard feet coming in a jog. It sounded as if it was one small person coming down the trail. Mookwig stood motionless beside the trail. When the small, old chief was directly in front of him, Mookwig dropped him with one swift blow from his club. He heard no one else except the three scrambling up the hill. He dashed off to catch them.

Just as Mookwig reached Bakting, the muscular chief threw himself from her back. Mookwig was on him like a hawk on a mouse. Tangtok leaped over Bakting. It took all the strength of the two friends to subdue the strong chief while muffling his mouth so he could make no noise. Fortunately, Dakwee had remembered to bring some rawhide strings. They tied the chief's hands behind his back and hobbled his legs close together so he could not run.

They continued up the hill and made no stops until they were at the upper end of the hidden meadow. They tied the chief to the small tree he was sitting next to with his back leaning against it. They tied a piece of hide over his mouth so he could not make any noise. They slept until Bright Light God woke them with his heat.

Mookwig approached the chief, made the hand sign of a chief, and tapped his chest, to confirm he was a chief. He made the sign for a young maiden and spread his arms apart with the palms up, the motion for a question, while asking, "Tiekee?"

The chief showed surprise at the name but shook his head to signal "No" or "Nothing."

This upset Mookwig because he knew the chief was lying. He went through those motions again and raised his voice in anger as he harshly questioned, "Tiekee?" The chief said nothing and tried to remain motionless, but his eyes flashed fear.

Tangtok asked Dakwee to help him gather vines to make a ring that they could place around Bakting's neck. They quickly made the ring, placed it over Bakting's head, and slid it back to her shoulder blades. On each side of the ring, he tied a long, strong vine as traces. He tied the traces to the chief's legs and then tied the chief's hands in front of his body. He told Mookwig to ask about Tiekee.

The chief flashed a look of bewilderment. He now realized that he was about to be dragged by Bakting. The chief signed to have the hide removed from over his mouth. Mookwig removed the hide. The chief started to talk but then stopped and clammed up.

Tangtok swung a leg over Bakting, and they took off in a gallop, with the chief bouncing along behind. They made two passes around in the meadow. When they stopped, the chief mumbled Tiekee's name and used some language that Mookwig understood. The chief eventually explained that Tiekee was in another village but he did not know where. Neither of the three who held the chief captive believed he did not know where she was.

They tied his arms to a stout tree. Tangtok eased Bakting forward. This stretched the chief a little. Mookwig asked, "Where Tiekee?' The chief shook his head signaling that he did not know. After Bakting took her third step forward and was leaning sharply into the ring of vines, the chief was wringing wet with sweat and showing great pain. As Tangtok was about to ask Bakting to take another step, the chief motioned to stop.

With Bakting still leaning into the ring of vines, Mookwig asked, "Where Tiekee?"

The chief mumbled, as well as he could, "I speak."

Tangtok allowed Bakting to ease back a little. The chief realized that he would be sent to the Silent Hole if he did not cooperate. He asked if Bakting was animal or spirit. Tangtok let him believe that she may be both. The bewildered chief then thanked them for not sending him to the Silent Hole.

He offered a blood oath with the three of them. Because they had saved him from the Silent Hole, and if they would promise to not let the "God Animal" Bakting stay in this area, he would have Tiekee delivered to them before Bright Light God slipped under the trees. He would have Tiekee on the trail one arrow shot upriver from the village. They all exchanged blood through pricked fingers. The chief left in a trot.

People who have integrity do not break an oath. The chief was an honorable man in his culture. He kept his word. While waiting for Tiekee, Tantok and Mookwig had a long, serious talk. Mookwig explained that all Tiekee talked about to him and his sisters was how could she ever become the squaw of Tangtok. Both accepted that the wise, old High Choptank Chief would suffer too much if he allowed his daughter to marry an Assateague. He would hurt for only a short time if his son married an Assateague and then became a chief of them. For certain, the old chief would then be happy to see his grandchildren thrive and grow up to be honorable people, no matter where they lived.

Mookwig and Dakwee agreed totally that Tiekee had her heart set on being with Tangtok. The three agreed that Tangtok should take Tiekee and Bakting to the land of the big sky country, where people knew cayuses. Mookwig and Dakwee would return to the island and ensure man and ponies would forever be friends.

The meeting with Tiekee was beyond describing. She had no idea why she was being led to this area on this trail. The first one she saw and recognized was none other than the brave of her dreams. She screamed and yelled, with tears of joy flowing down her flushed and beautiful cheeks. She dashed from the group around her and sailed into the strong arms of the one she loved so deeply.

After the joyous, raucous greetings, Mookwig said to Dakwee, "We go." They left together in a swift walk going down the trail, heading home.

Just before getting out of sight, they turned and looked back. Their last view of family, friend, and pony was a young, strong brave walking beside his beautiful squaw riding comfortably on a pony of Assateague, disappearing over a ridgeline, facing directly into Bright Light God, as He silently slipped under the tree line. They were heading toward the lands of the Comanche and other cayuses.

What Big God joins together, let no Brave, Maiden or pony rip apart.[8]

GLOSSARY

Alien: belonging to another place, a stranger

Big God: the one God

Big Water: the Atlantic Ocean Bright Light(s): one or more days

Bright Light God: the sun

Cayuse(s): horse(s)

Copse: a small group of trees

Cold season: winter

Cuddy: a small room on a ship

Feather-white-hard-water: snow

Hacienda: Spanish for ranch

Hot season: summer

Little Water: Chincoteague Bay

Muscadines: southern grapes that flourish in the wild

Pocosin: flat, swampy woods in the coastal areas

Pale-Face: a white person

Pale-Face Light God: the moon

Pale-Face Light(s): twenty-eight days between full moons

Papoose: baby

Powwow: an American Indian ceremony, meeting

Scat: feces, manure

Silent Hole: death

Two-legs-no-feathers: people

Two-legs-with-feathers: birds

White Silent Hole: freeze to death

ENDNOTES

[1] Herd of ponies. https://search.aol.com/aol/image?p=assateague+island+ponies&sit=img-ans&v_t=webmail-searchbox&fr=webmail-09/23/19

[2] Spanish galleon. http://www.lostshipofthedesert.com/spanish-galleon-an- dalucia/09/22/2019

[3] Powhatan village. https://shorturl.at/EKKzq

[4] Pony & water. https://www.tripsavvy.com/wild-horses-and-ponies-of- the-southeast-1639501 09/22/2019

[5] American Indian canoe. https://shorturl.at/DswJw

[6] One of many jingles sang circa 1945 by the local blacks, including the late John Henry Emory, Sr., Old Chapel Station, west of Square Farm, Chapel Road, Easton. MD.

[7] Paraphrased and based upon Exodus 14:13 KJV * * *" ye shall see them again no more forever." Also, Nez Perce Chief Joseph, when surrendering to the Army in Oct 1877, used a form of the phrase, above, when he stated, "From where the sun now stands, I will fight no more forever."

[8] A paraphrase of Matthew 19:6 (KJV).

ABOUT THE AUTHOR
Major (retired) Bill Spies (Spees)

Bill was born February 02, 1935 and raised on a farm on the Eastern Shore of Maryland. He captained a skipjack dredging oysters under sail on the Chesapeake Bay, and served twenty-two years in the US Army. He has led in the Infantry as: Fire-team Leader, Squad Leader, Platoon Sergeant, Platoon Leader and Company Commander. Bill served as a Captain in the 7th Infantry Division G-3 Staff and as Commandant, 7th Division Counter-guerilla Warfare School, Korea. He served as an Airborne and as a Ranger Instructor at Fort Benning, GA.

During his Army terminal assignment, he served as Operations Officer (S-3), Ranger Department, for thirty months and then simultaneously for twenty-two months as Commanding Officer, Benning Ranger Training Division (now the 4th Airborne-Ranger Training Battalion), and as the Assistant Director, Ranger Department, US Army Infantry School, Fort Benning, Georgia.

His awards and decorations include: Legion of Merit, two Bronze Stars for Valor, two Purple Hearts; the Combat and Expert Infantry Badges; the Pathfinder, Master Parachutist, Jungle Expert badges; and the coveted Ranger Tab. He is a member of the Army Ranger Hall of Fame and is a Distinguished Member of the Airborne-Ranger Training Brigade. He was honored as the "2017 Spirit of Infantry" recipient.

Bill has led an 1,100-acre farm operation, a heavy-equipment construction company and was a Real Estate Qualifying Broker. He earned a Bachelor of Science degree, Business Management, from Troy State University, Phenix City, AL. He is a successful author of LEADER = WINNER, which explains how to effectively teach, train, test, grade, critique, and counsel leadership. He accepts the universal, nondenominational church of God of the Holy Bible. Bill resides with his wife, Donna, in Fort Mitchell, Alabama.